Joy

By Danielle Steel

JOY · RESURRECTION · ONLY THE BRAVE · NEVER TOO LATE · UPSIDE DOWN
THE BALL AT VERSAILLES · SECOND ACT · HAPPINESS · PALAZZO
THE WEDDING PLANNER · WORTHY OPPONENTS · WITHOUT A TRACE
THE WHITTIERS · THE HIGH NOTES · THE CHALLENGE · SUSPECTS · BEAUTIFUL
HIGH STAKES · INVISIBLE · FLYING ANGELS · THE BUTLER · COMPLICATIONS
NINE LIVES · FINDING ASHLEY · THE AFFAIR · NEIGHBORS · ALL THAT GLITTERS
ROYAL · DADDY'S GIRLS · THE WEDDING DRESS · THE NUMBERS GAME
MORAL COMPASS · SPY · CHILD'S PLAY · THE DARK SIDE · LOST AND FOUND
BLESSING IN DISGUISE · SILENT NIGHT · TURNING POINT · BEAUCHAMP HALL
IN HIS FATHER'S FOOTSTEPS · THE GOOD FIGHT · THE CAST · ACCIDENTAL HEROES
FALL FROM GRACE · PAST PERFECT · FAIRYTALE · THE RIGHT TIME · THE DUCHESS
AGAINST ALL ODDS · DANGEROUS GAMES · THE MISTRESS · THE AWARD
RUSHING WATERS · MAGIC · THE APARTMENT · PROPERTY OF A NOBLEWOMAN
BLUE · PRECIOUS GIFTS · UNDERCOVER · COUNTRY · PRODIGAL SON · PEGASUS
A PERFECT LIFE · POWER PLAY · WINNERS · FIRST SIGHT · UNTIL THE END OF TIME
THE SINS OF THE MOTHER · FRIENDS FOREVER · BETRAYAL · HOTEL VENDÔME
HAPPY BIRTHDAY · 44 CHARLES STREET · LEGACY · FAMILY TIES · BIG GIRL
SOUTHERN LIGHTS · MATTERS OF THE HEART · ONE DAY AT A TIME
A GOOD WOMAN · ROGUE · HONOR THYSELF · AMAZING GRACE · BUNGALOW 2
SISTERS · H.R.H. · COMING OUT · THE HOUSE · TOXIC BACHELORS · MIRACLE
IMPOSSIBLE · ECHOES · SECOND CHANCE · RANSOM · SAFE HARBOUR
JOHNNY ANGEL · DATING GAME · ANSWERED PRAYERS · SUNSET IN ST. TROPEZ
THE COTTAGE · THE KISS · LEAP OF FAITH · LONE EAGLE · JOURNEY
THE HOUSE ON HOPE STREET · THE WEDDING · IRRESISTIBLE FORCES
GRANNY DAN · BITTERSWEET · MIRROR IMAGE · THE KLONE AND I
THE LONG ROAD HOME · THE GHOST · SPECIAL DELIVERY · THE RANCH
SILENT HONOR · MALICE · FIVE DAYS IN PARIS · LIGHTNING · WINGS · THE GIFT
ACCIDENT · VANISHED · MIXED BLESSINGS · JEWELS · NO GREATER LOVE
HEARTBEAT · MESSAGE FROM NAM · DADDY · STAR · ZOYA · KALEIDOSCOPE
FINE THINGS · WANDERLUST · SECRETS · FAMILY ALBUM · FULL CIRCLE
CHANGES · THURSTON HOUSE · CROSSINGS · ONCE IN A LIFETIME
A PERFECT STRANGER · REMEMBRANCE · PALOMINO · LOVE: *POEMS* · THE RING
LOVING · TO LOVE AGAIN · SUMMER'S END · SEASON OF PASSION · THE PROMISE
NOW AND FOREVER · PASSION'S PROMISE · GOING HOME

Nonfiction

EXPECT A MIRACLE: *Quotations to Live and Love By*
PURE JOY: *The Dogs We Love*
A GIFT OF HOPE: *Helping the Homeless*
HIS BRIGHT LIGHT: *The Story of Nick Traina*

For Children

PRETTY MINNIE IN PARIS · PRETTY MINNIE IN HOLLYWOOD

Danielle Steel

Joy

A Novel

Delacorte Press | New York

Joy is a work of fiction. Names, characters, places, and incidents are the products of the author's imagination or are used fictitiously. Any resemblance to actual events, locales, or persons, living or dead, is entirely coincidental.

Copyright © 2024 by Danielle Steel

All rights reserved.

Published in the United States by Delacorte Press,
an imprint of Random House,
a division of Penguin Random House LLC, New York.

DELACORTE PRESS is a registered trademark and the DP colophon is
a trademark of Penguin Random House LLC.

LIBRARY OF CONGRESS CATALOGING-IN-PUBLICATION DATA
Names: Steel, Danielle, author.
Title: Joy : a novel / Danielle Steel.
Description: New York : Delacorte Press, 2024.
Identifiers: LCCN 2023034725 (print) | LCCN 2023034726 (ebook) |
ISBN 9780593498613 (hardcover ; acid-free paper) |
ISBN 9780593498620 (ebook)
Subjects: LCGFT: Novels.
Classification: LCC PS3569.T33828 J69 2024 (print) |
LCC PS3569.T33828 (ebook) | DDC 813/.54—dc23/eng/20230825
LC record available at https://lccn.loc.gov/2023034725
LC ebook record available at https://lccn.loc.gov/2023034726

Printed in the United States of America on acid-free paper

randomhousebooks.com

2 4 6 8 9 7 5 3 1

First Edition

To my beloved children,
Beatrix, Trevor, Todd,
Nick, Samantha, Victoria
and Vanessa, Maxx and Zara,

May you always have joy in your lives,
and love and courage,
and kind people to share their joy with you.

It's a light in you that is always there.
Cherish it, it is a precious gift to share.
I love you with every ounce of my being,

Mom/d.s.

"Real isn't how you are made," said the Skin Horse. "It's a thing that happens to you. When a child loves you for a long, long time, not just to play with, but REALLY loves you, then you become Real."

"Does it hurt?" asked the Rabbit.

"Sometimes," said the Skin Horse, for he was always truthful. "When you are Real, you don't mind being hurt."

"Does it happen all at once . . . or bit by bit?"

"It doesn't happen all at once," said the Skin Horse. "You become. It takes a long time. That's why it doesn't often happen to people who break easily, or have sharp edges, or who have to be carefully kept. Generally, by the time you are Real, most of your hair has been loved off, and your eyes drop out and you get loose in the joints and very shabby. But these things don't matter at all, because once you are Real you can't be ugly, except to people who don't understand."

—"The Velveteen Rabbit"
by Margery Williams

Joy

Chapter 1

Allegra Dixon could remember perfectly the day her mother left. She was six years old. Anna, the housekeeper, was off. Allegra's mother, Isabelle, usually slept late, and her father, Bradley, was home from one of his long trips. She had learned early on not to bother them and to make as little noise as possible. She was tiptoeing down the stairs to get something to eat for breakfast, and she heard her parents talking in the kitchen. They were speaking loud enough for her to hear them before she entered the room. She wasn't sure whether to go in or not, so she stopped to listen.

Her parents didn't shout. They were polite to each other. When Allegra's father wasn't home, her mother laughed a lot. Allegra thought her laughter sounded like bells. Isabelle was exquisite. She had long red hair, green eyes, and a beautiful face. She wore fancy dresses and jewelry, and perfume that smelled delicious. When Allegra's father was away, her mother went out almost every evening, and the housekeeper would stay with her until her mother came home. They lived in Washington, D.C., in a house in Georgetown. Isabelle often went to New York to see her friends, and Anna would stay then too. Isabelle's parents, Allegra's grandparents, the Vander-Holts, lived in New York.

Her father was in the army. He wore a uniform and was very handsome. He went to faraway places and stayed a long time, sometimes even a year. He went to places like Libya and Liberia in Africa, and South America. He only came home from time to time. When he was home he worked at a place called the Pentagon. He hardly spoke to Allegra, and when he did, he never seemed to know what to say. He would ask her about school, or tell her how much she had grown since he'd last seen her, which had always been a long time.

Their voices in the kitchen sounded serious that day. Her mother wasn't laughing. Allegra heard her say that she was going back to New York. Her father asked her what she expected him to do with "the child." He usually referred to her as the child and seldom used her name when he spoke about her, so she assumed the question was about her. He said he would be leaving again in two weeks. Isabelle said that Allegra could stay at the house in Washington with Anna. She couldn't take a child with her. She was planning to stay with friends. Allegra's father said that was impossible. The child needed at least one parent with her, and Isabelle said she wasn't going to be it.

Allegra tiptoed away quietly, deciding it wasn't the right time to enter the kitchen. She was frightened and confused. Her heart was beating fast. If her mother was leaving and couldn't take her, and her father was going away again, and she couldn't stay alone in Washington with Anna unless she had a parent with her—what was

Joy

going to happen to her? What did it mean for her? She hardly ever saw her paternal grandparents, and they were very old. Her mother had said her parents weren't an option either. Allegra went back upstairs to her room and sat on her bed with her teddy bear in her arms. His name was George. She had to wait for them to tell her where she was going.

When she walked back to her room, Allegra saw her mother's suitcases lined up outside her bedroom. She'd seen her packing the day before. Her pretty dresses had been laid out on her bed. Allegra guessed that she was going to a party in New York. She always took a lot of clothes with her, but this time she was taking even more.

Allegra sat quietly on her bed for a long time, waiting for them to come to see her. She wasn't hungry anymore. She heard a car come then, and voices downstairs. She heard footsteps on the landing. They came and went for a little while, and then the front door closed. The car drove away, and no one came to her room to see her.

Her father didn't come up for a long time. She waited all day. They had forgotten her. They did that sometimes when they were busy. And then the door opened and her father walked in. He was wearing his uniform and he looked very serious. He looked at her sitting on her bed with the bear in her arms. He stared at her for a minute. She was a tiny miniature of her mother, with the same red hair and green eyes. Possibly an unwelcome reminder now. Then finally, he spoke.

"Your mother's gone away," he said in a solemn voice. He hesitated for an instant and then added, "She's not coming back." He waited, not knowing what else to say, and then he turned around and left and closed the door softly behind him. He had forgotten that there was no one in the house to feed Allegra, since it was Anna's day off. It didn't matter. Allegra wasn't hungry anyway. She sat looking at the door, holding George tightly in her arms. Her father hadn't told her where she was going, or if she was going anywhere. She had no idea what was to become of her. All she could think of was that her mother had forgotten to say goodbye when she left. Her father always told her to be brave, so she didn't cry, in case he came back to her room. But he didn't. She curled up into a ball on her bed, holding George, until she fell asleep.

The briefly torrid affair between Bradley Dixon and Isabelle VanderHolt had lasted months, and the marriage seven years. Everything about it was improbable. She was a Golden Girl, a dazzling young debutante-turned-socialite in New York, the wild child of the ultra-respectable VanderHolts. At eighteen, after graduating from an exclusive private girls' school in New York, she had no interest in college. She had fallen in with the fashionable underground elite of the city, with Andy Warhol and his entourage. She was a nightly regular at Studio 54, known as "a modern day Gomorrah," a hotbed of drugs and disco, socialites mingling with musicians, Hollywood stars, and a hefty dose of appealing riffraff. The ambience was racy and unsuitable. Her parents had long since given up trying to rein her in. She was their only child. A trust fund set up by her paternal grandparents gave her total autonomy at twenty-one. Her parents couldn't stop her. She was beautiful and young and wild, with Rita Hayworth looks and a body to match. She'd been paired with various inappropriate people, including her friends at Warhol's Factory.

Joy

She'd made cameo appearances in several of his films, more beautiful than any movie star. She was twenty-one when she met Bradley Dixon.

It was 1979, and Colonel Bradley Dixon, much decorated hero, veteran of Vietnam, had spent the last four years, after the final skirmishes in Vietnam, in Laos, Cambodia, and various trouble spots in Africa. High-ranking in the Military Intelligence Corps, he'd played an important role in the signing of the peace in Vietnam. He was forty-three years old the night he walked into Studio 54 with friends, wearing black tie and not his uniform, and saw Isabelle. It wasn't his usual scene, but his friends insisted he go with them. They said he needed to loosen up. They weren't wrong. He had lived in the military all his life. Only son, only child of four-star general Tom Dixon, Bradley had grown up all over the world. He had graduated from West Point and had trained for military intelligence early in his career. He'd married an army brat like himself, the daughter of another high-ranking officer. The marriage fell apart while he was in Vietnam for extended tours of duty. His career always came first and wasn't compatible with marriage. His wife had divorced him while he was gone, and eventually married someone else, another officer with a tamer and less illustrious career. Bradley had no children with her and had never remarried. One had to make choices in life. His first love was his career, until he met Isabelle that night.

He had spotted her as soon as he walked into Studio 54, a dazzling redhead dancing wildly with a famous Black singer. She saw Bradley too, handsome in black tie. He had two drinks and asked her to dance. They danced for hours, and he left her at Studio 54 and went back to his hotel, bewitched by her. He was based in Washington, D.C., for a few months, and came to New York often to see her. They were married in six months. She was twenty-two years old and he was forty-three. Her parents were dubious about the match, and about her ability to settle down. Bradley's father wasn't enthused about Isabelle either. Everything about her spelled trouble, starting with her looks, her friends, her history, her freedom.

They had Allegra quickly, an unwelcome surprise. The baby startled Bradley with how sweet she was, the rare times he was home. Isabelle was not the kind of woman one left quietly sitting by the fire, or with a baby in her arms. She spent more time with her friends in New York than with her baby when Bradley was gone. He was well aware that he couldn't control his wife and stopped trying early on.

In the seven years of their marriage, he had been sent all over the world, to every trouble spot on the map. Panama, the Middle East, Libya, Korea. Isabelle toned down her social life on Bradley's brief visits home, as much as she was able, and stayed in Washington with him, but the pull to Warhol and his cohorts and her other friends in New York was strong. She could hardly conceal her relief whenever Bradley left. She was dazzled by him when they met, but got bored with him quickly. It was no secret that she wasn't cut out to be a military wife, and never even tried. She hated the other army wives, and they didn't like her either. She lived and played by her own rules. She was part of another, fancier, more social world. She had thought he was strong and sexy, and discovered too late how cold he was, though fabulous in bed in their early days.

Their daughter, Allegra, was an unfortunate mistake. As soon as Bradley left town, so did Isabelle, going back to New York. She stayed with friends. Her life never slowed down, nor did his. She was deeply embedded in the fast life in New York. Living in Washington never kept her at home, it was a convenient place to leave the child with their housekeeper or a nanny or babysitter, whoever she found to stay with her. Isabelle's parents never interfered. They knew better. Isabelle did what she wanted. Bradley's parents recognized how wild she was and felt they were too old to get involved. They had no other grandchildren and saw very little of Allegra. Children made them uncomfortable. Bradley's father was in his seventies by then, still involved with the Department of Defense. Their son's fascination with Isabelle was beyond their comprehension. She was anything but a wife or mother.

In spite of a thousand reasons not to, Bradley hung on to the marriage. He didn't want a second divorce, but he wasn't home enough to fix the marriage or try to get Isabelle in line. He could handle military maneuvers of a thousand men or ferret five hundred guerillas out of the jungle better than he could manage one wife like Isabelle. He had loved her in the beginning, but that gradually waned. She was like a wild horse one loved to own but couldn't ride. And Allegra became a forgotten bystander, an observer of her parents' unraveling marriage. Bradley wasn't surprised when Isabelle said that she was leaving and that he no longer loved her. The problem was the child. He had no idea what to do with her, and Isabelle flatly refused to take her. She had never wanted to be a mother.

It took him two weeks to convince his parents to let Allegra stay with them, at least until he returned to Washington again. He had no time to make other arrangements, and they agreed to let her come for a few months. It wasn't an ideal arrangement. They weren't set up to care for a child and weren't enthused about it, but Bradley knew she'd be well cared for and safe, so he insisted. They lived in upstate New York on the Hudson, near West Point, in healthy surroundings for a child. The night before she left, Bradley told Allegra where she was going. She was packed up and taken there a few days before he left. Isabelle had already made it clear to him that she didn't want custody and would let him know when she could manage visitation, but certainly not now. At twenty-nine, free of him and Allegra at last, the wild horse had been let out of the barn and was about to run free. She was leaving for London shortly, another scene that suited her even better. Her London friends were just as racy as those in New York.

General Thomas Dixon and his wife, Carol, welcomed Allegra with their usual reserve. They weren't accustomed to children, and hadn't seen Allegra often in her six years. Bradley rarely had time to see them between trips and Isabelle never bothered. They were shocked by Allegra's mother abandoning her and leaving their son with the burden of caring for her, since he traveled easily ten months of the year, if not more. They were proud of his career, but much less so of his marriage. Bradley hadn't heard anything from Isabelle's parents since she'd left and he didn't expect to. They weren't avid grandparents either, and Isabelle saw little of them. She had worn them out in her youth, they had no patience for her, and they avoided her as much as possible. They were constantly afraid of a scandal, and were not pleased at the idea of a divorce either.

Joy

* * *

When Allegra arrived at her grandparents' home in upstate New York with her two suitcases, driven there by her father three days before he was due to leave, she had no idea how long she was going to stay there. Nor did Bradley. His parents said they would see how it worked out. They thought she was too young to be separated from both parents, but there were simply no other options. Anna hadn't wanted to leave Washington. She had a fiancé there, and Bradley's parents didn't want a stranger underfoot in their home. Bradley had told Allegra she had to behave, which she normally did anyway. She was an extremely quiet child, and respectful of adults.

The Dixons' home was big and joyless and institutional-looking. It was near the Academy. Bradley had made arrangements for Allegra to go to a local school. The public school was good there. A school bus would pick her up every day. All his parents had to do was feed her and house her, and they weren't planning to do much more than that. They had a cook and a housekeeper, and Bradley's mother said the help could babysit for Allegra when necessary. None of them saw this as a long-term arrangement. It was a stopgap measure for as long as Bradley was away.

His assignment was due to last eleven months. To their surprise, Allegra was as little trouble as Bradley had said. She was like a little ghost living in their midst. They never saw her. She stayed in her room most of the time, much to their relief. Their two employees fed her and kept an eye on her. The cook took Allegra to a Disney movie at Christmastime, and the housekeeper picked all the Christmas gifts the Dixons planned to give her. There weren't many. Allegra was used to emotional deprivation even before she arrived, so she made no demands and had no expectations. She had a rich fantasy life in the loneliness of her grandparents' home. She read all the books she could. Her father came to visit when he returned from his assignment, and by then it appeared that the arrangement was working, and his parents agreed to let her stay. Bradley had let the house in Georgetown go when Isabelle left and got an apartment instead, so it didn't matter how long he was away.

Bradley was back for a month and only had time to see Allegra twice. West Point was a long way from Washington, D.C. Anna had married and moved away by then, so he had used a service to keep his apartment clean during his absence and had no one who could have taken care of Allegra while he was home. He was at meetings night and day, preparing for his next assignment. Isabelle was still in London, and he hadn't heard from her in several months. Their divorce had already been filed and was in its final stages, giving sole custody to Bradley, with Isabelle's full consent.

Allegra was used to living with her grandparents by then. She loved spending time outdoors and being in the country, and she liked her school. She wasn't allowed to bring friends home. There was no reason to change what was working, and Bradley still had no better solution to suggest. Isabelle's parents had made it clear to him that they couldn't possibly take on a child Allegra's age.

Allegra lived with her paternal grandparents for five years, making herself as small as she could in the rigid, chilly atmosphere of their home. At first she had tried to win them over and be loving and help-

Joy

ful. Overt signs of affection made both her grandparents uncomfortable, and they discouraged them. Bradley visited her there when he was home, but she never lived with him again. After Isabelle left him he was assigned to Libya, the Persian Gulf, Panama, and Liberia, and was rarely back in the States for long.

Allegra enjoyed visiting West Point whenever her grandfather took her there to observe maneuvers or see a parade. She thought it was exciting, and it reminded her of her father. All the men in their uniforms looked a little like him to her.

Her grandparents had taken her to see her mother twice in five years, when Isabelle was in New York visiting from London, where she had settled. Allegra thought Isabelle was as beautiful as ever, and was bowled over when her mother hugged her. She was so starved for affection that she felt a rush of love for her the moment she did. She had become accustomed to the austerity of her grandparents, who spoke to her as an adult and never touched her. When she hugged her father, he always stiffened, and she knew she'd done something wrong. There was nowhere to go with the love she had inside her, no one to give it to. It lay dormant within her, like a deep well filling up from an unknown source. She still slept with her teddy bear at night, which her grandmother disapproved of, but allowed.

Allegra loved seeing her mother the two times she did. Isabelle was so exquisite and so exciting. She was easy to love and to hug, and Isabelle let her. She was soft and smooth, and her perfume smelled delicious. She still wore the same one. Allegra always remembered it. Allegra spent a day with her, and then, like a butterfly, her mother flew away, and the brilliant colors of her wings disappeared from Allegra's world. She had gone somewhere to see her friends, and Allegra went back to upstate New York with her grandparents to the drab world there. Her grandparents' worst fear was that she might turn out like her mother, and they did everything they could do to discourage that and ensure that she grew up to be a responsible, serious person, with "normal" values. Bradley tried to encourage that too on his rare, brief visits.

The five years of almost military austerity ended suddenly when her grandmother had a stroke and died, and her grandfather, with advancing senility, was unable to take care of Allegra or himself. Bradley had to make other arrangements for both when he came home for his mother's funeral. There was no other solution than to put Allegra in an excellent private boarding school. At eleven she was old enough by then, in his opinion. The school had male and female sections, and served as a feeder school for West Point. Bradley had attended high school there. He told Allegra she would love it. And once again, there was no other option.

Bradley had just begun a tour of duty in the Persian Gulf region and was expecting to be away for at least a year. For the first time, he turned to Isabelle's parents for help. They had offered none so far. They sent her token Christmas gifts, some sweaters and books, and once a doll. They were old but still very social. At Bradley's insistent urging, they agreed to let Allegra spend Thanksgiving and Christmas with them, as well as whatever time she didn't spend at a camp he put her in for the summer in Maine.

The VanderHolts weren't equipped to care for a child, but when they saw Allegra, they were reassured. She was extremely subdued. She knew what was expected of her from her years with the Dixons.

Joy

She was to make no demands, act like an adult, keep a respectful distance, and be invisible, and she was good at it. She read voraciously, staying in her room during her visits to them. Her only escape from her loveless existence was in books. She was a package whom the adults in her life passed to each other with reluctance and restraint. Isabelle had long since decided to stay in England, and she told Bradley that sending Allegra to her was unthinkable. She had no time for her daughter, and even she admitted that her life was unsuitable for a child. Bradley could guess that was true and didn't question it or insist.

Bradley went back to the Gulf, and Allegra began her seven-year sentence in boarding school. She was a diligent student and a bright girl. She had her father's fine mind and her mother's looks. It was a winning combination. Her teachers liked her, and she made a few friends, but she was retiring and shy after years of feeling unwelcome wherever she was, and it was embarrassing, not having a family when the other students spoke of theirs. They had brothers and sisters, parents and grandparents, aunts and uncles, cousins and friends, people they spent their school holidays with and had had a life with previously. Allegra had had an absentee father for her entire life, a mother who had abandoned her at six. Her paternal grandfather had died within a year of his wife, when Allegra was twelve. She didn't see him after she left for boarding school. She had attended the funeral, with all the pomp and ceremony due a four-star general. There was no way she could explain all that was missing from her life. She always felt that somehow it must be her fault. If she had been more lovable, or met their expectations better, or maybe if she looked less like her mother, they would have liked her better, or even loved her. She was too young to understand that her father's and her grandparents' failure to express love to her was due entirely to their inability to love anyone. Her mother was so narcissistic that the only person she was able to love was herself. Her six years of motherhood had been more than enough for her. Allegra got letters from her occasionally in response to hers that were like letters from a distant friend, not a mother. Isabelle abhorred the role of mother and avoided it at all cost.

Her maternal grandparents faced Allegra's initial visits with dread, terrified that she would become as uncontrollable and unruly as her mother had been, which was far from the case. Sensing their reluctance to have her there, she only came out of her room for meals. They lived on Fifth Avenue in New York and had a "cottage" in Newport, Rhode Island. It was one of the great homes, a vast marble mansion as cold as they were, but a spectacular place that looked like a museum. They spent holidays and vacations there. The house was very grand, filled with valuable objects and art. They had a large staff and Allegra had dinner in the kitchen with the servants, who were very kind to her, while her grandparents were out almost every night with equally social friends, or when they entertained them at home in black tie, and she was too young to be included, much to their relief.

Allegra had tea with her grandparents once or twice a week. They would talk to her about school. They gave her gifts on Christmas and her birthday that had been picked by the housekeeper, and at the end of the school vacation, she gratefully went back to boarding school. At least she had somewhere to go for holidays, but she never felt welcome or as though she belonged there. She was the inter-

Joy

loper in their midst. They were fulfilling a duty they felt obliged to perform, forced into it by her father. As time went on, she realized that her father had shamed them into having her spend her school holidays with them. They were the only family she had, other than her father, who was on the other side of the world most of the time, and a mother who had no interest in her whatsoever. Essentially, Allegra was alone in the world. Her father visited her at boarding school when he came to the States. He never stayed long, as he was very busy at the Pentagon. They were strangers to each other and always had been. The walls he had built between them were too high to scale now. Allegra accepted the boundaries he set.

Allegra was sixteen the summer she met Shepherd Williams, a tall, handsome, bright boy with dark hair and blue eyes. His parents and grandparents spent the summers in Newport in a cottage almost as large as the one she stayed at. His grandparents knew hers. His family were very proper, traditional Bostonians. Shepherd was twenty and attended West Point, which was familiar to her. He had two older brothers he wasn't close to and who were considerably older, both married and living on the West Coast. She and Shep became fast friends. He told Allegra he wasn't sure he wanted to make a career of the army, but his parents had convinced him that West Point offered him a good education in the meantime. And his grandfather had gone to West Point. Shep had doubts about West Point, since he didn't want a military career. He was sensitive and thoughtful and very smart. He and Allegra became good friends and confidantes, and felt like soulmates. He had never had a friend like her.

He could tell her anything, and she could pour her soul out to him. He was fascinated by her. She said whatever she thought and was unfailingly honest but never unkind. She was a gentle person. Knowing him changed her life. She shared the ideas and feelings with him she had never been able to express with anyone. They wrote to each other between summers, and saw each other at Christmas in New York or in Newport.

Their friendship deepened into love the summer she was eighteen. She had been accepted at Columbia and was starting college in the fall, and he had just graduated from West Point as a second lieutenant, and not knowing what else to do, he had decided to stay in the military. Allegra's father didn't attend her high school graduation. He was in Afghanistan and the Sudan, but promised to spend Christmas with her. Her grandparents had come to her graduation. It was awkward but she felt it was nice of them to come. She felt grown-up now that she was about to enter college.

She and Shepherd became lovers that summer, and her heart poured out all the love she had to give him, love she had waited a lifetime to give someone. It was a tender relationship, and he was a sensitive young man. He wanted to go into military intelligence, like her father, "but only for a while." He was about to start a basic officer leader course for a year in Washington, D.C., and would then lead a military intelligence unit. He had five years of active duty ahead of him. Allegra warned him that military life and the army would swallow him up and eat him alive. He promised that would never happen. She had seen what her father's military career had done to him. He was ice cold and seemed almost inhuman. She had

Joy

come to recognize that her father was incapable of allowing himself to have feelings for another human being. He had been dutiful toward his parents, but not affectionate, nor were they to him. He had been disappointed by two women, and Allegra sensed that she was an unfortunate reminder in the flesh of one of them. She looked more like her mother with every passing year, without the wild exuberance and flamboyant behavior, but their physical traits and beauty were strikingly similar. By burying himself in his career, Bradley had kept himself from deep and lasting attachments, even to his only child. He looked pained every time he saw her, and almost frightened that some emotion would surface that he didn't want to deal with. As she got older, she read about the wars he was involved in, and realized that he must have seen unimaginable horrors in his job. She feared that for Shepherd. He thought he could deal with it, but few people could. They either turned into robots, like her father, or they shattered inside, into a million broken pieces.

Shep's paternal grandfather had been military, but his father was in business, and although they weren't warm people, they were more accessible than her family, and polite to her. Her mother's family, the VanderHolts, had made a lifetime career of social engagements and superficial values, and were selfish and self-centered more than anything. Her father's family, the Dixons, were encased in ice. By the time she turned eighteen, from a lifetime of observation, she understood it. She didn't want anything like what had happened to her father to happen to Shepherd. He was a deeply sensitive person, which was what she loved about him. The Military Intelligence Corps would send him to trouble spots all over the world, which could ruin him, as it had her father. She didn't know if her father had ever been a warm person, but he certainly wasn't now. Or for as long as she could remember.

"I'm not going to stay in the army long enough for that to happen," Shep reassured her. "I'll do my five years' active duty in intelligence and get out. And the reserves after that. You have to stay in active duty for a lot longer for it to break you."

"That's not always true. Who knows how many wars it takes in uncivilized places before that happens? Why don't you try to quit sooner?" she suggested naively, and he smiled.

"That wouldn't be honorable. Besides, they don't let you. I owe them the next five years after West Point. And at least intelligence is interesting."

"That's what I'm worried about. I just don't want them to break you by the time you get out."

"Trust me, they won't. I won't let that happen. It's going to work out just fine. Right about the time you graduate, I'll be almost ready to get out of the army, and then we can decide what to do next." He had it all figured out, and she hoped he was right. She wasn't as confident as he was that he could escape the damage that being in military intelligence could do, depending on where they sent him. But they both still had a long way to go. She was just starting college at Columbia, and he had military intelligence training to get through and his own unit to run. He was going to be based in Washington, D.C., for several years, at George Washington University, which brought back memories for her. She hadn't lived in Washington since her mother left, but she still remembered it fondly.

Shepherd had promised to visit Allegra frequently in New York.

Joy

That would be fun too. She was looking forward to being a grown-up, being able to make her own decisions, and not being sent to relatives who didn't want her around. She wanted her own life now, and she had been lucky enough to meet a boy who actually loved her. It was the first time she could remember ever being loved. She had a lifetime of unspent love to give Shep, like money in the bank that had been piling up and accruing interest. She had never been so happy in her life as the summer of 1998 drew to a close.

Chapter 2

The timing worked out perfectly. Shepherd didn't have to report for training in Washington until three days after Allegra had to be at Columbia in New York to move into her dorm and sign in for orientation. He drove her down from Newport with a van full of what she had been buying all summer. Her father had sent her an allowance for supplies, and was paying for her college education, just as he had paid for boarding school and all her incidentals and expenses. It was the only thing he had ever done for her—he felt it was his responsibility to pay for her education, and the basics she needed for school and college and her life in New York now. To Shep, she called it "blood money" that her father gave her so he didn't have to be there. He paid his dues without complaint and was a virtual father.

Shep helped her set up her stereo and carried in her trunk for her. He did everything everyone else's father was doing, and they went out to dinner at night. They had spent every minute together that summer, and it was going to be strange not being with him when he left for Washington. Her grandparents thought it was a harmless flirtation, and didn't realize it had gone farther than that, nor did his very conservative Bostonian parents. None had any objections to their spending time together, assuming it would fade away once she went to college and he went to Washington, although they had been close friends for two years by then. Their families didn't take their relationship seriously. At eighteen and twenty-two, Allegra and Shepherd had their whole lives ahead of them for serious attachments and to meet the right people, according to their families. Their elders dismissed it as a passing fancy, a summer romance, with no understanding of how bonded they were. Shepherd had always felt like the odd man out in his family. Ten and twelve years younger than his brothers, who lived far away and rarely came home, and with older, extremely proper, rigid parents, he had nothing in common with them. And Allegra understood him and had no family attachments at all.

Shep and Allegra had already talked about the future, and they both knew that this was the real thing. They didn't argue with their families about it. It was easier if they didn't take it seriously. They might have worried about it otherwise, that their relationship would distract them from what they had to do, with the army and school.

It took Shep two days to set everything up for her at Columbia, and he stayed an extra day just to be with her. He even went to orientation with her. She was excited about Columbia and Shep was happy for her. She was free now.

"I'm going to miss you," she said on their last night together. He

Joy

was staying at a small, inexpensive hotel on the West Side, and she spent the night with him there, saying she was staying with her grandparents when she signed out at her dorm. She had met her two roommates, but didn't know them well yet, and didn't owe them any explanations. They were busy with their parents. For once, she didn't care that she didn't have parents to be there with her. Her father was in Iraq and had promised to be home by Christmas. She wasn't counting on it, and if he didn't make it back, she and Shep had agreed to spend the holidays together in either New York or Newport, depending on where their grandparents were, so they could stay with them respectively and see each other.

Allegra and Shepherd left the hotel early the next morning, so he could take the train to Washington and she could get to her first class. He had promised to come back that weekend if he could get away, or the following one. Unlike everyone else in her life, Shepherd never disappointed her, especially since they had become lovers that summer. He spent every moment with her he could, and never let her down. They were both looking forward to their classes that fall—his leadership course and then military intelligence training, and her studies in English lit at Columbia. With Shep stationed in Washington, there would be lots of opportunities for weekends together. They were both good students and Allegra had to keep up with her assignments, papers, and exams, and there was so much to learn, for both of them.

In reality, they managed a surprising number of weekends together during her freshman year in college. Shep joined Allegra and her grandparents for Thanksgiving dinner in New York. His older brothers were going to their in-laws' that year, and his parents had decided to take a cruise, which left him at loose ends, so he was grateful to spend the holiday with Allegra and the VanderHolts. The weather had been particularly snowy in Rhode Island, so they decided not to go to Newport. Allegra always thought it was more fun in the summer, and she enjoyed New York in the winter.

Predictably, her father didn't make it back from Iraq for Christmas. It neither surprised her nor mattered to her. She liked her roommates but wasn't close to them. She was used to keeping her distance, except for Shep. They were closer than ever. He had a long leave, and both their families went to Newport for the holiday, so they were together there, and they went skiing in Vermont afterward, each of them pretending to go with friends. They stayed at a romantic little inn Shep paid for. She chipped in for meals and bought a cheap pair of secondhand skis.

It had been a perfect Christmas for Allegra, better than any that had come before, because she was with Shep. Her father was promising to return to the States in May, but she knew how hard it was for him to predict his schedule. If they got word in Iraq of any planned subversive activity, he'd have to stay. She never counted on seeing him at the time he said. It was the nature of his work.

Allegra had a Christmas card from her mother with a check for two hundred dollars in it, and a note telling her to buy herself a present. It was a first. She used it to pay for the secondhand skis. She wondered if her mother could guess that George, the teddy bear, still sat on her bed. For too many years, he had been Allegra's only confidant and friend. Now she had Shep. They told each other every-

Joy

thing, talking late into the night, whether on the phone or in person. They never ran out of things to say or confidences to share. They had both had lonely childhoods. Shep had suffered from cold, distant parents. His brothers had both left for college when he was still a child. He was six and eight years old when they left. His older brothers were close to each other and not to him. He had been a late accident of their parents, and most of the time he felt they all acted as if he didn't exist. He was an embarrassment. Allegra's situation was more extreme, with two absentee parents, and grandparents who were never comfortable with having her with them. Isabelle had exhausted them with her wild, unruly behavior, and having a teenager in the house at all created a negative déjà vu for them, even if she was well behaved. They were relieved that she was in college now and didn't want to stay with them for long. They had done their duty for seven years as holiday grandparents, and were delighted that she was growing up. They approved of Shepherd because they knew his grandparents from Newport, and he was from a respectable Boston family of bankers.

"Do you realize that everyone we're related to is a snob?" Allegra said to Shep one night. He laughed. "If you were from some regular family, and didn't have a house in Newport, my family wouldn't like you. That's disgusting."

"It's how those families work. They feel safer with their own kind. And your grandmother may approve of me, but she doesn't talk to me. My family isn't fancy enough, and their house isn't big enough to impress her, and I don't think she likes the fact that I'm from Boston." Allegra knew it was somewhat true. Her grandparents were fancier than his, and wealthier, which mattered to them too.

"And your mother always comments that my father is a soldier. But so was her father-in-law, and now so are you."

"She forgives me everything because I'm her son." He smiled at Allegra. He couldn't help noticing how beautiful she was. He felt like the luckiest man in the world because she loved him. They were very attractive young people and made a handsome couple.

"I think she thinks my father is a murderer, since he's career army. And she's probably right," Allegra said, she hated to think about it. She was sure she would be horrified at the things her father had done, if she knew about them. But she never would. She didn't want Shep to go down that path. It would destroy him. But he said he was enjoying his military intelligence classes, though he couldn't talk about them. It was the only thing in his life he didn't discuss with Allegra. They were like two bodies with one soul.

Her sophomore year went just as smoothly, and the following one. Her classes were getting more interesting. Her relationship with Shep had grown deeper. At the beginning of her senior year, they had been lovers for three years, and best friends for two years before that.

Shep had another two years to complete on active duty, and four weeks off during the summer, which he spent in Newport. Allegra stayed at her grandparents' house to be near him. They were inseparable. She was twenty-one and he was twenty-five. She had hardly seen her father for the past two years. He was the head of military intelligence in Iraq. He was sixty-five years old and planned to retire at sixty-eight. He was a lieutenant general, with a presidential deferment to stay on active duty until his sixty-eighth birthday. And then

Joy

he had to retire. But the military was his life, and he was vital and strong. The army needed him, for his expertise and experience. He was stationed in the Middle East as Allegra began her senior year at Columbia. Shepherd was working full-time in military intelligence in Washington, and enjoying the job, but he was still planning to leave the army in two years, a year after Allegra graduated. Their plans dovetailed perfectly, and had for all her college years.

The most shocking thing that had ever happened to either of them occurred shortly after her classes started in September. She was in New York and Shep in Washington the morning the planes hit the Twin Towers, on September 11. Her class was dismissed immediately and she rushed home to her apartment to see the news on TV. She saw the report that the Pentagon had been hit in Washington, and she was panicked for Shep. At first, she was afraid a war was starting. What actually was happening was so shocking no one could understand it at first. She saw the Twin Towers come down and cried as she watched. It was hours before she could reach Shep, and a week before she saw him, when he finally could come to New York.

Whatever insider information he had, he couldn't share with her. The entire country was badly shaken, and New York was somber and subdued. It was a full month before the city returned to a semblance of normal and people seemed in better spirits. Shep told her that life would never be the same, after an attack on American soil that was so devastating.

In October, a month after 9/11, they were making plans for Thanksgiving when Shep showed up in New York on a Tuesday night without warning. He always called to tell her he was coming. Allegra had her own small student apartment by then, near school, which her father paid for. Shep had a key and let himself in. She was studying and suddenly looked up and he was standing there. He looked pale and troubled.

"What are you doing here?" she asked, as she stood up to kiss him, and he put his arms around her.

"I need to talk to you," he said as they both sat down.

"Do you want something to eat?" He shook his head. She knew something had happened, and she could feel a chill run through her. "What's wrong?"

"I got orders today. They're sending me to Afghanistan," he said, with a tormented look in his eyes.

"I thought they were going to keep you in Washington?" She frowned, shocked by the news.

"That's what they said. They changed their minds. They can send me wherever they want. And I have the training for this." He had never said that before.

"Is this because of 9/11?" she asked him, and he nodded. "Can you refuse to go?" she asked, feeling breathless and reaching for his hand. He held it tightly in his as they sat on the couch in her apartment. The assignment had come as a shock to him too.

"No. I'm in the army. I'd have to have a damn good reason, like health, not to go, and I don't. They're only sending me for six months, and then I've got another eighteen months in Washington before I finish active duty."

"You can't go." Allegra looked desperate. She had seen what places like that had done to her father. In her opinion, Bradley was subhuman, no matter how good he was at his job, or probably because of it. She didn't want that happening to Shep. They would ruin him. He was the gentlest soul she knew. He would never survive a war zone like that, and the things that happened there. She knew enough about military intelligence from her father to be terrified for Shep.

"I don't have a choice," he explained to her. "These are orders, not an invitation. I'll be attached to MI while I'm there. In theory it's a strategic office job." They had trained him for a situation like this one.

"There's no such thing in a war zone. Everyone gets pulled in to do the dirty work, and in places like that, it couldn't be dirtier." Allegra had read a lot about it. "When do you have to go?"

"In three weeks," he said, still holding tightly to her hand. He had wanted to tell her in person. He couldn't give her news like that over the phone. He knew how upset she would be. He was too, but there was nothing he could do about it. He had to go.

"You won't be here for Thanksgiving," she said, feeling as though she was in a haze and had lost her sense of direction.

"I know."

"Or for Christmas. When would you come back?"

"In May," he said in a flat voice. It sounded like a lifetime away to both of them. If he didn't get shot or killed in the meantime.

"What do we do now?" she asked him, still feeling dazed. She felt as though a wrecking ball had hit them.

"I want to get married," he said in a strained voice.

"Now?" She hadn't expected that.

"Before I go. I feel like it will protect me." What Shep said brought tears to her eyes. "And we want to get married anyway." And they had always said they didn't want a big social wedding. Allegra nodded, thinking about what he'd said. She liked the idea too. It would confirm everything they felt for each other, and had for five years. They had grown up together.

"Do you want a real wedding and all that?" she asked him, to be sure. That would be harder to pull off. Her grandfather had been ill recently, and her grandmother was getting frail and was not up to planning a wedding, if she would even do it. Allegra had always figured she'd have to plan her own wedding one day, even a small one, and three weeks wasn't enough time to do it. The fanfare didn't matter to either of them, it never had. All they cared about was being married to each other.

"No, let's just go to City Hall and do it. We could get the license tomorrow before I go back. And we'll get married this weekend. I think you have to wait a couple of days after you get the license."

She nodded agreement. "I'll skip my early class tomorrow. Are you going to tell your parents?" she asked him. She wasn't sure if they would approve or not. They still thought she was too young for such a serious relationship.

"I don't know. If I tell them, they'll want us to wait and have some big deal wedding in Newport. We can always plan that later. This is just about us, if you want to do it," he asked shyly. It was a big step for both of them.

"I do want to," she said seriously. Everything was moving so quickly. "My grandmother will think the same thing. Let's not deal with everyone's opinions, and just do it." He smiled at her answer and wasn't surprised. They were always on the same page, soul-

Joy

mates. She hoped that their being married would protect him from the evil forces he'd be fighting every day, the dangers of a war zone, especially in that part of the world. Her father was there. She wondered whether she should tell him Shep was arriving, and if they'd be in the same place. Maybe Bradley could look out for Shep, although she doubted he would. He had no paternal instincts for her or anyone else.

They lay awake talking for most of the night, and finally fell asleep. It was still dark when they got up early, went out, rode the subway downtown, and were at the front of the line, waiting to get into City Hall when it opened. They went straight to the Bureau of Licenses and filled out the forms. They got the license and Allegra put it in her purse for safekeeping. He kissed her and they felt like two conspirators on a secret mission, and then he took the subway to Penn Station to catch his train to D.C., and she went all the way back uptown to Columbia. It was exciting knowing that she had their marriage license in her purse. Marrying Shep was the most important thing she'd ever done in her entire life. It would change everything. She'd be a married woman, and one day they'd have children. This was the beginning, and when he came back, if they wanted to, they could have a proper Newport wedding in the Vander-Holt mansion, to please their families and make it seem more official. But this seemed much more real. She would be his wife when he left, and for the rest of their lives until one of them died.

She was glad that he wanted to get married. After classes that afternoon, she called her father in Afghanistan. He had an office there, if he was in it, and not touring around the countryside on a mission. She wasn't calling to tell him she was getting married. She wanted to tell him that Shep was coming to Afghanistan, and to look out for him. He was surprised to hear from her—she never called him, except to wish him a happy birthday, or on Christmas.

"Is everything all right?" he asked her in a businesslike voice. He knew her grandfather hadn't been well recently.

"Yes and no," she said in a serious voice. "Shep is being sent to Afghanistan in three weeks. I wanted you to know."

"I'll find out where they're sending him. Maybe to my office, or he may get assigned to some other detail. They keep the MI boys busy here out in the field. We catch a fair number of spies we have to deal with," he said matter-of-factly, which filled her heart with fear again.

"I wish they weren't sending him. He has less than two years left."

"We all wind up in places like this at some time. He's had a soft ride till now. Afghanistan will make a man of him." Shep already was a man, and the last thing she wanted was for him to turn into a man like her father. His notion of manhood was very different from hers. They talked for a few more minutes, and he said he'd find out when Shep arrived and look him up. He liked him better knowing he was being given an assignment in a hard post, instead of a desk job at the Pentagon.

Allegra didn't tell Bradley she was getting married in three days. It was a private matter between her and Shep, and she had no desire to share it with her father. One day, he would walk her down the aisle in his dress uniform, which was just window-dressing. The real heart of their marriage was being born at City Hall in three days, and Bradley had no place in that. He had shared none of her joys and sorrows over the years, and this was going to be the most important moment in her life. She wanted to share it with Shep, and no

Joy

one else. He was the only person who had been there for her in her entire life. Her grandparents had been shamed into grudgingly hosting her for holidays, and her father had never been there for her at all. She owed him nothing, except to be polite to him when he visited her for a few hours once every year or eighteen months.

Shep arrived at midnight on Friday. His current job in military intelligence was a standard office job, five days a week, with evenings and weekends off. He had taken the train from Washington after work, as he had almost every weekend for three years. Everything had been so easy until now. And now he had to face Afghanistan.

They were among the first on line at City Hall. Allegra had worn a white wool dress she already owned, and a white coat she had bought that week with her allowance, and they lent her a bouquet at City Hall. She had worn her red hair straight down her back, and she looked beautiful and young. Even in the institutional surroundings, there was a sudden magic to it when the City Hall employee performing the ceremonies that day pronounced them man and wife and Shep kissed her. They had none of the trappings of the kind of wedding they would have had, but it was a moment they both knew they would cherish forever. Allegra handed back the bouquet when they left, and they walked out into the October sunshine. It was a glorious autumn day in New York.

"What'll we do now?" she asked him, beaming. For a moment, they forgot the reason for their hasty marriage, and were just a young couple with their whole life together ahead of them. Shep had a plan, and he hailed a cab. He had the driver take them to the

Plaza Hotel, where he handed Allegra into a white hansom cab, and after they took a tour of Central Park, the carriage driver took them down Fifth Avenue to the 21 Club. They had both eaten there with their grandparents at various times but had never been there together. Shep had reserved a table for them and ordered champagne. They toasted each other, had a sumptuous lunch, and afterward went back to her small student apartment uptown.

In spite of the circumstances and no one to celebrate with them, Shep and Allegra turned it into a special day. Even when they went back to her apartment, it felt different than usual. He carried her over the threshold, and they made love with all the tenderness and poignancy of the day. He fell asleep in her arms afterward, and she watched his beautiful face as he slept. There had always been an innocence to him which touched her deeply. Sometimes he was more like a boy than a man. There was still a playful, childlike quality that she loved about him, and he brought that out in her as well.

It was chilly that night and they snuggled in her bed, and when he woke up, they talked about the things they had done in Newport the summer they met. The memories would have to keep them going for the next six months after he left. They tried to forget the reason for their hasty marriage, but it was always there, a drumroll in the distance, a storm ready to engulf them. They would have to hold on tight to get through it. They were both ready to do that. It was painful to realize that once he left, she wouldn't see him again until May. It seemed an eternity away. They had never been apart for that long since they'd met.

On Sunday, they went for a long walk in the park. She smiled every time she looked at the narrow gold wedding ring he had put

Joy

on her finger the day before. He had bought it in Washington and brought it with him, and had borrowed a ring of hers without her knowing so he would get the right size. He was wearing a wedding ring too. He hadn't decided yet if he was going to tell the army he had gotten married. If he did, her father might find out, and Allegra didn't want Bradley to know. He would be annoyed that they hadn't waited to do it properly, with a full guard of West Point cadets holding crossed swords over their heads, worthy of a West Point officer. She knew the kind of wedding her father would have wanted for her. He hadn't been there for a single important moment in her life, but he would want all the pomp and ceremony due his rank, which she didn't care about. She couldn't remember the last time he had hugged her, and yet he would want to give her away. The hypocrisy of it was jarring.

It was enough to be married to Shep. She didn't need to tell the world. One day they would, at the right time, with Afghanistan behind them.

He took the early train back to Washington on Monday morning, and was pensive all day, thinking about her and their wedding weekend and what it meant to him. He didn't see how he was going to be able to leave her in a few weeks. He would receive rigorous combat training once he got to Afghanistan, although he wasn't supposed to be in combat, being in military intelligence. But situations happened, and he had to know the local style of combat and what he might run into unexpectedly. He hadn't said anything to Allegra about it. It was just part of the drill of going to the area.

He went to New York every weekend until the last one, and then she went to Washington. She skipped some classes to see him off.

She wanted to be with him until the very last minute they would be able to share.

Their last weekend together was hard. The minutes ticked by so loudly you could almost hear them, like sand filtering down an hourglass. Second by second, she was losing him, and wondered who would come back in his place. She knew that the worst wounds that returned from war were those you couldn't see.

He had to go back to the base the night before he left. She dropped him off in a car they had rented, and he held her tight before he got out of the car.

"Don't worry, I'll be back, Mrs. Williams." He savored the name and she smiled. She loved the sound of it. She kissed him and he touched her face, as though trying to remember the feel of her, her touch, the tenderness of her lips on his.

"Just come back to me the way you are," she said softly. "I'll be waiting for you, Shep."

"I know you will." He finally had to force himself to let go of her and get out of the car. He stood looking at her for a moment, smiled, and then walked toward his barracks, with a last wave at her.

As she watched him disappear, she felt her whole body shudder, knowing that tomorrow he would be in Afghanistan, and there was nothing she could do to protect him there. All she could do was pray that he'd come back to her sane and whole and alive.

She took the car back to the garage where they'd rented it. He had already paid for it, and she took a cab to the station. She caught the last train back to New York. She was his wife now. She sat huddled in her seat on the train, and stared out the window into the night, as

Joy

all the images of the past weeks flooded into her mind. She couldn't lose him now, she thought. Life couldn't be that cruel to them.

It was too late to call him when she got home that night. He would be gone in the morning when she woke up. He'd be on his way to Afghanistan. She touched the wedding band on her finger and prayed that their love would keep him safe, and he would come home to her the same man who had left.

Chapter 3

The winter without Shep was hard for Allegra. She tried to occupy her time with schoolwork. She had her senior thesis to write. She had chosen to do it about the hidden themes in Shakespeare, which was an ambitious subject, but working on it filled her winter nights. She spent Thanksgiving with her VanderHolt grandparents, and was sad to see for the first time that her grandfather was confused. She'd never noticed it before. Arthur was seventy-nine years old, and had seemed fine until then.

Her grandparents stayed in New York for the holidays, and Allegra spent Christmas with them. Her grandmother, Mariette, inquired about Shep, and when Allegra said he was in Afghanistan for a six-month tour of duty Mariette was surprised to hear it.

Allegra had letters from Shep regularly and he called her when he could. He sounded tired when he called, and he said conditions there were rigorous and worse than he'd been told, but he didn't offer any details. She didn't know if he meant living conditions for the officers and troops, or the state of the war. He had seen her father once, and they'd talked for a few minutes. He said her father appeared to be thriving, which didn't surprise her. Being sent to war zone posts always revitalized him. She wondered if he'd ever retire. But she was more concerned about Shep. He sounded discouraged in some of his letters, and said he couldn't wait to come home.

She spent spring break in the library at Columbia, working on her thesis. She would be graduating in May and had to finish it. Shep was more than halfway through his tour of duty by then, and she was counting the days until he came home. She smiled whenever she looked at her wedding band on her finger. When she visited her grandparents, she always wore another ring that obscured it, but the rest of the time it was the only piece of jewelry she wore. It reminded her of the promise of their marriage and better times to come, when they wouldn't be separated.

They were holding up under the strain, and she wrote to him almost daily, sharing all her thoughts in his absence and telling him what she was doing. She wrote about the few friends she saw when she wasn't studying, only one or two knew she was married. He said her letters were keeping him going and meant the world to him. He had taken a stack of photographs of her with him, and he looked at them constantly. He thought she was the most beautiful woman in the world. She smiled whenever he said it. She didn't believe him, but it was nice to hear, and to know that he felt that way.

At Easter, Allegra's grandfather had a bad fall. He slipped getting out of the shower and broke a hip. It needed surgery, and the operation

Joy

didn't go as smoothly as they hoped. Allegra dutifully went to see him, and he looked as though he had aged ten years. She noticed that his confusion had gotten worse. He kept thinking she was her mother and calling her Isabelle. Allegra thought Arthur was young to have dementia at seventy-nine. And for the first time, she felt sorry for her grandmother. She was distraught about her husband, and afraid to lose him. Allegra went to have dinner with her a few times, and tried to reassure her. Mariette complained that Isabelle had only called twice to see how her father was and hadn't come to New York to see him.

"She's got to be the most self-centered woman in the world," Mariettte commented, surprisingly lucid, and then looked at Allegra. "Why am I telling you that? She was completely irresponsible as a mother, and she's never been much better to us as a daughter. It didn't matter so much when we were younger, but it does now. Your grandfather keeps asking for her, and I keep reminding him that she's in London, and I say she's busy. But there's really no excuse for her not calling him. And it wouldn't kill her to show up in New York once in a while. All she thinks about is going to parties. She hasn't changed since she was a young girl. She's forty-four years old, and you'd think by now she would have settled down. That man she's been dating for the last year sounds no better than she is. They go to hunts and parties and balls all over Europe. I read about her in magazines more than we hear from her." They were all the reasons she had abandoned Allegra fifteen years earlier. Isabelle's parents were equally social and superficial in their own snobbish way, but they had never abandoned their daughter, she had abandoned them, and their marriage had been solid for fifty years. They had celebrated their golden wedding anniversary the year before and given a big party in Newport for their friends. They had invited Allegra, and she had gone with Shep. Her grandmother had worn an elegant and subdued gold dress by Oscar de la Renta.

Her grandfather's situation didn't improve. He came home from the hospital and caught bronchitis, which turned into pneumonia.

Allegra went to visit them and was shocked at her grandfather's condition. He looked like he had lost twenty pounds, and he didn't recognize her. For the first time, she had genuine feelings for them. Her grandmother looked desperate. Arthur had around-the-clock nurses, and on Easter Sunday, he slipped away and died in his sleep.

Her grandmother called her to tell her the news, early on Easter morning, and Allegra dressed hastily and took a cab to their apartment. Mariette was sitting in her bedroom, bereft, wearing a plain black dress, and suddenly looked a hundred years old, although she was only seventy-four. It made Allegra aware of how much Mariette had loved him, and it reminded her of how heartbroken she would be if something happened to Shep.

She helped her grandmother make the arrangements. She called the funeral home and wrote the obituary for her. There wasn't a great deal to say about her grandfather. Arthur VanderHolt had been an investment banker for many years and had retired fourteen years before. He belonged to all the right clubs in New York and had gone to Princeton. He had no outstanding accomplishments. He came from an aristocratic family but didn't have a huge fortune. He and Mariette had money, but he wasn't famous, he was just well known in the blue-blood social circles they moved in. The obituary Allegra wrote said that he was of New York, New York, and Newport, Rhode

Joy

Island, and was survived by his widow, Mariette Ashton VanderHolt, a daughter, Isabelle VanderHolt of London, and a granddaughter, Allegra Dixon. She had written "beloved" husband and father, had hesitated for a long time, staring at the page, and had finally added the word "beloved" before grandfather. It was her final tribute to him. He had never been particularly interested in her, and Allegra remembered how reluctant he and Mariette had been to have her visit from boarding school when she was eleven, and how chilly they had been to her, having her eat with the staff in the kitchen. But in the end, they had been reasonably decent and faithful grandparents to her for the past ten years. Their affection for each other had grown over time, and they had never turned their backs on her as her parents had. In fact, they were shocked by how little her father saw of her, and much more so by their own daughter, who had abandoned a six-year-old, had never mended her ways, and had made no attempt to make amends or get to know Allegra.

Mariette realized now that Allegra was a lovely young woman with far better morals and values than her mother had, and who had never had the benefit of any affection whatsoever from her parents. Mariette thought it was appalling and was ashamed of her own daughter for having neglected Allegra all her life. She thought it was a wonder Allegra had turned out so well, no thanks to Isabelle. Mariette regretted now not having spent more time with Allegra when she was younger, and was touched that Allegra didn't hold it against them.

"Isabelle says she's coming to the funeral," Mariette said to Allegra in a small voice over tea that afternoon. She looked drained. It had been the worst day of her life. "It's the least she can do. She hasn't been to visit us in almost four years. She's always too busy, and your grandfather hasn't wanted to travel for the last five years. She could have come to see us. She's arriving the night before the funeral, and only staying for two days. Ever since her great friend Warhol died, she's not interested in coming to New York. I think he died the year after she left your father. That's when she moved to London. The party was over for her here." She spoke in a disapproving tone, and Allegra didn't comment. She knew from her father that her mother had been part of that whole scene, although he didn't speak of it often, and hadn't in years. He never mentioned Isabelle anymore.

True to her word, Isabelle arrived the night before the funeral, and stayed at the Carlyle. She arrived at the apartment two hours before the funeral in a chic black Chanel suit, with a big black hat that made her look incredibly glamorous, and she was wearing big dark glasses. In spite of herself, Allegra was excited about seeing her. She had seen so little of her mother in her life that Isabelle was like the Ghost of Christmas Past appearing, and Allegra was fascinated by her. At forty-four, she was strikingly beautiful, and had an ease and grace about her. She hugged her mother, and then Allegra, and blew a kiss into the air.

Allegra had worn a plain black dress, a black coat, and high heels, and had done her red hair in a simple bun. She didn't have a black hat to wear. She looked plain and beautiful, with very little makeup, just some mascara and pale pink lipstick. The resemblance between mother and daughter was still striking. They looked as if they could have been sisters. Years before, Allegra might have questioned her mother about why she had removed herself so totally from her life, and if she regretted it, but this wasn't the time. It was obvious that Isabelle had no regrets. She looked happy and at ease as she floated around the room like a butterfly, as she always did. She asked if there was anything she could do to help, but it was much too late for that. Allegra and her grieving grandmother had done it all by then.

"Allegra helped me," Mariette said sternly, in a tone of reproach.

"What a good girl," Isabelle said with a smile at her daughter, and Allegra noticed that she was wearing a large diamond solitaire on her left hand. Mariette noticed it a few minutes later.

"What's that?" she asked bluntly.

"I'm engaged," Isabelle said, looking sultry and coy. "Hubert finally proposed. We're getting married this summer on a friend's boat in Saint-Tropez. I'm not sure I'm cut out for marriage, but after three years, we know each other well. We're kindred spirits. He's never been keen on marriage either."

"At least you won't be having more children," her mother said tersely, in defense of Allegra.

"Hubert has five. That's more than enough. Fortunately, they all live in South Africa. They never come to England. His ex-wife is South African. She took them all back to Cape Town with her when they divorced, ages ago. He's not close to any of them," she said, with obvious relief.

"And that's something to be proud of?" Mariette said, angry at her daughter again. Allegra had remained silent.

"It makes life simpler," Isabelle said with a sigh, glancing at Allegra. There wasn't a trace of guilt in her smile. "Your grandparents have taken good care of you," she said breezily to Allegra. It was a statement and not a question. In fact no one had taken care of Allegra, or her emotional needs, for her entire life, which her mother didn't know or care about. Isabelle was a rare and most unusual breed, with no maternal instincts whatsoever.

It was almost time for the funeral then, and Mariette went to put on her hat and coat. She was wearing a small black hat with a veil, no jewelry, and a black mink coat, since there was still a chill in the air. Isabelle went to straighten her hat and put on some lipstick, and Allegra stood by to help her grandmother, and put on her plain black coat, which hung shapelessly on her. It wasn't chic or beautiful, but it was respectful, which her grandmother appreciated.

"I'm sorry," her grandmother whispered to her, as Allegra helped her with her coat. "She never changes. It's who she is." Allegra nodded, still somewhat taken aback by how blithe her mother was about her lack of interest in children, even and perhaps especially her own. She wasn't in the least apologetic about it.

They rode in the limousine to the church together. The hearse was already there, at St. Ignatius Loyola on Park Avenue, and the casket was at the altar. Many people were already seated when they walked in, and there was soft organ music playing. Copies of the program Allegra and her grandmother had put together, with the photograph Mariette had chosen of her husband, were sitting on the pews. Allegra noticed several people recognizing Isabelle.

The service began shortly after they arrived and was simple and respectful. It wasn't showy but it was dignified and elegant. There were lilies and orchids on the altar and the casket, and in two large urns, and the flowers people had sent were set up around the altar.

Joy

The guests paid their respects to a man who had been unexceptional but who had been a good friend to many of them. He had been well liked in his community and at his clubs. Allegra noticed that the caretakers of the house in Newport were there. She was sorry Shep couldn't be there too.

Mariette and Isabelle spoke briefly to several people after the service. None of them paid attention to Allegra. She had always been the invisible child, and most had never talked to her. They were dazzled by Isabelle, as she had intended. She liked being the star of the show.

Caterers had set up at the apartment for a small reception afterward, and Allegra had called her grandmother's close friends for her. They came to the apartment and stayed for an hour or so. And as soon as they left, Isabelle went to change, reappeared in a black pantsuit she had brought with her, and announced that she was meeting friends for dinner. She said she assumed her mother was exhausted and would want to rest, and she kissed her and waved at Allegra. She didn't ask Allegra to join her, and Allegra wasn't surprised. Isabelle left in a cloud of perfume with her red hair down, and Mariette looked at her granddaughter and shook her head.

"I don't know why I always expect her to be different. I thought she'd grow up eventually, but she never has. She will be a beautiful butterfly forever. I don't think she's ever loved anyone in her life. I hope her new husband knows what he's getting into. From all I hear, he's much the same. Thank you for helping me to put the service together, Allegra. It was beautiful. Your grandfather would have loved it. It was dignified and perfect."

"Thank you." Allegra smiled at her. She felt sorry for her grandmother. Life as she had known it was over. It wouldn't be the same for her without her husband, and she knew it. She was mourning both the man and the life they had shared, which had brought them both a great deal of pleasure, but would be entirely different now for Mariette, alone. "You should try to get some rest," Allegra said gently, and her grandmother nodded, and went to her room a few minutes later to lie down. Allegra went to her own room and took off the ugly black dress and put on jeans and a sweater. She was thinking about Shep. She would be graduating in seven weeks, and he was due back two weeks later. His tour of duty in Afghanistan was almost over. They had survived it. It hadn't been easy, but they had gotten through it, and had remained in constant contact. She was sure that there were things he wasn't allowed to tell her, but even if he sounded stressed at times, and even disheartened, he seemed okay.

Allegra saw her mother again the day after the funeral, when she came to visit Mariette. She spent an hour talking to her, and went through some papers and photographs of her father her mother wanted her to see. Mariette had come across them while looking for the photograph for the funeral program. There was a particularly nice photograph of Isabelle and her father at her coming-out ball. She was in a beautiful white dress. She looked spectacular and her father was very handsome. He was a very distinguished-looking man. He'd been about fifty-four years old in the picture, and Isabelle was eighteen. She had married Bradley Dixon only four years later. Between the two events she had gone wild with the Warhol crowd,

Joy

and at Studio 54. She often said those had been her best years, and surely the most fun. Twenty-five years later, she was still having fun.

Isabelle showed the photograph of her debut to Allegra, who looked at it admiringly. She could see the resemblance, but her mother was so much more flamboyant and extroverted. She radiated excitement and joy. Allegra was a much quieter person, with a much more peaceful nature. She would never have dared to be as exuberant as her mother. She had been forced to hide all her life from people who didn't want her around, or to nurture herself when they left her to her own devices or abandoned her like her parents. She had never had the luxury of being as sure of herself as Isabelle was. She couldn't even imagine what that would feel like. Allegra had been forced to be invisible for most of her life, in order to avoid getting hurt or rejected.

"Studio 54 was fantastic," Isabelle said to Allegra, with the light of memory in her eyes. "It didn't last long, but it was fabulous. People really had fun then. The world is a lot quieter and more boring now."

"Maybe fewer drugs," Mariette commented, and as Isabelle laughed, Allegra heard the sound that had reminded her of bells as a child. She remembered that and the scent of her exotic perfume most of all.

"I used to love your perfume," Allegra said with a dreamy expression.

Her mother smiled at the memory. "I wore two in those days, Femme by Rochas and Shalimar by Guerlain. I blended them myself. I don't wear either of them anymore. It's funny that you remember that." She looked touched for a moment. Allegra didn't say that she had so few memories of her mother to hang on to that her perfumes stood out, and they had been very distinctive. She hadn't smelled them on anyone else since, and in her memory they belonged to her mother.

Isabelle stood up to leave a little while later, and said she had a lunch to go to. She was meeting some old friends.

"I'm flying back to London tonight," she said. She was wearing a white skirt with a black jacket and looked very chic again, and sexy in very high heels. She had terrific legs, and Allegra realized that she had the same ones, but never showed them off with short skirts and stiletto heels the way her mother did. Allegra had noticed that Isabelle's shoes had red soles. Everything about her was noticeable and striking, while everything about Allegra was soft and subtle. Her mother wasn't warm. She was a showpiece that would attract attention anywhere, which was what she wanted.

Allegra left her mother and grandmother alone for a few minutes, in case they wanted to say a private goodbye. She was always careful not to be intrusive, and despite her close blood relation to them, she and they were strangers to each other. She came back to the living room five minutes later and didn't see Isabelle. She looked puzzled, and glanced at her grandmother for an explanation.

"She's gone," Mariette said with a look of resignation. "She flits in and out. She's a steel butterfly. She looks delicate but she isn't. She's as tough as nails and she always gets what she wants."

"I wanted to say goodbye to her," Allegra said, looking bereft for a minute. Isabelle's departure brought back a flood of memories of

Joy

waiting on her bed all day, holding her teddy bear. And history had just repeated itself. Once again, the woman who was her mother, and didn't want to be, had forgotten to say goodbye. Or maybe this time she hadn't forgotten, she just didn't want to. Goodbyes were much too complicated for her, and required emotions she didn't want to feel.

"That's how she is," Mariette said quietly. "God knows when I'll see her again." Allegra was thinking the same thing. Maybe never. Once every five or ten years, Isabelle blew in on a gust of wind and flew away just as quickly. Her grandmother was right. She was a steel butterfly, with a heart of stone.

Allegra's heart only bled for a few minutes this time. But she remembered so clearly for an instant how she had felt that day, sitting on her bed, waiting for her mother to say goodbye to her, and her father to tell her what was going to happen to her, holding on to George, her teddy bear, for dear life. Now, Isabelle had forgotten to say goodbye again. It was a clear message of how little her daughter meant to her. But this time, Allegra didn't care as much. She had Shep. He was her husband, and he was coming home in two months.

Allegra graduated from Columbia in May, alone. Her grandmother had said she'd come, but she called Allegra early that morning and said she just wasn't feeling up to it. Mariette hadn't felt well since her husband had died, and she had hardly gotten out of bed since the funeral. She was afraid that if she went, she might faint and cause a scene. Allegra said she understood, and hung up the phone. Shep had called the night before to wish her luck. He felt terrible that she had gone through her grandfather's funeral without him, and had seen her mother. She told him that Isabelle had forgotten to say goodbye. It was almost ironic this time, sixteen years later. Allegra had just turned twenty-two.

The ceremony was very moving, and she got her diploma. She threw her mortarboard cap in the air like everyone else. There was no one there to celebrate her, and it didn't matter. She was with her classmates, had gotten her degree, and could look for a job now. She had already sent her résumé to several publishers. She wanted to be an editorial assistant. Books had always been important to her.

After she returned the gown she had rented, and the cap once she retrieved it, she kept the tassel as a souvenir. She had handed in her senior thesis on time before graduation. Her father sent her a telegram congratulating her, so at least he had remembered, and her grandmother had given her a nice check the week before.

After the ceremony, all the students went out with their parents. There were parties all over the city, and in student apartments. Graduates were moving out of the dorms, and others were packing up for the summer. Apartments like hers were being vacated. Allegra was keeping hers for when Shep came home. He was going to move to New York with her when the army released him, and go back and forth until then. They had their whole lives ahead of them, and everything to look forward to.

She got calls for two interviews in the weeks after graduation, and the day she and Shep had waited for finally came. He had been delayed for a few days, and she went to Washington to meet him. He was due in on a flight the morning after she took the train to Washington. She stayed at a hotel near the base where she'd stayed be-

Joy

fore. She was waiting in the visiting area at the time he had given her, and then she saw him, loping toward her with his familiar gait. She couldn't even see his face yet, but she would have known the way he walked anywhere. As she approached him, she started running, and flew into his arms the moment she got to him. He had grown a mustache, which made him look older, and she could see how thin he was. His eyes looked sunken when she backed away a few inches to take a look at him after he kissed her. He clung to her as though he was drowning and couldn't let her go. There were tears in his eyes and on her cheeks when he kissed her again. It was a moment she knew she would always remember as he held her. There was something unbearably sad in his eyes, but he was smiling. She could tell that he had seen things he never should have, but he was home now, he was alive, and he was safe. Whatever he had seen, she would help him forget.

"Welcome home, Shep," she said softly, as he held her.

"There were times when I thought I'd never see you again," he whispered, and she knew it was the truth from the way he looked when he said it.

"I was here, waiting for you," she said, as he put an arm around her shoulders and they walked slowly toward where she'd left the car she had rented. He wanted to drive to New York with her, he didn't want to take the train. He wanted to be alone with her. The hard, lonely months melted away as they looked at each other, and she smiled.

"Let's drive up to Newport tomorrow. We can stay at my parents' house. There's no one there yet," he said. He had three weeks of leave before he had to be at the intelligence office in Washington. He didn't have to be back in Washington until then. He wanted to see the ocean and smell the air. He wanted to put everything he'd seen behind him and be with Allegra.

"We can do whatever you want," she said peacefully. Everything in her life seemed perfect now that he was home.

"I have to see my parents. We can go to Boston in a few days. I want to be alone with you first."

"When are we going to tell them that we're married?"

"Whenever you want, Mrs. Williams." He grinned at her, and she saw in his smile the boy she had fallen in love with when she was sixteen. His eyes were the eyes of a man who had seen too much pain and suffering in the past six months, and had suffered himself. His face was thinner, but there was still something boyish about his face and the way he looked at her. He was twenty-six years old now, and she was twenty-two. Best of all, she was his wife, and he had come back to her safe and alive and whole. They hadn't destroyed him, and he was hers again, to have and to hold, forever.

Chapter 4

Driving to New York, she felt like she was dreaming and was afraid that she'd wake up and he'd be gone. He let her drive, and they stopped to buy food along the way to eat in the car, and got to New York in the late afternoon and returned the car. Allegra's building was quiet since the students who lived there were gone by then, and the apartments would remain empty until August when they all came back. The building seemed eerie and deserted without them. Allegra unlocked the door, and they walked in. Shep looked around as though he had landed in Paradise. His eyes had that faraway look again that he had had when she first saw him. He seemed as though he was coming back from a distant place, different and worse than anything she could have imagined.

There were no words to tell her what he'd seen in the past six months. He didn't want to. He didn't want her to ever know what it had been like. They had lied to him again and again. They lied to him every day, and then he saw the truth when he went on the missions he was assigned to. The things they did to people, and that people did to them. The torture that was part of every interrogation, that was standard procedure there. He had talked to Allegra's father about it when he'd seen him, and Bradley had laughed at him and said, "Toughen up, son. You're not in Kansas anymore. This isn't *The Wizard of Oz,* it's real life. And it doesn't get realer than this." He said it as though he enjoyed it, and Shep had known then that they would never be friends. Bradley Dixon was an animal, and he stayed in the army at whatever age he was to satisfy his bloodlust and his need for excitement. The interrogations gave him an adrenaline rush. Shep had been in on one of them with him, and had thrown up afterward for hours. All he wanted was to live long enough to go home to Allegra. Now he was home, and for the first time, he couldn't talk to her, because he couldn't tell her what it was really like, and didn't want her to know about her father, although he knew that she suspected it, and had for years.

Allegra didn't respect her father. She didn't even like him. He had gone over to the dark side years before and never came back. There were plenty of others like him there, and he was the leader of the pack. It was why, Shep knew now, he never came home for long, because he couldn't live in the civilized world anymore. He could only exist in the nightmare they had created, he was part of it. Shep didn't want to be one of them, but he had been for the past few months. It was like an initiation into some kind of satanic cult, and he had been one of them while he was there, and he didn't want Allegra ever to know what he had seen and done.

It had nearly cost him his soul, and now he was home, and she

Joy

was so clean and pure and whole he was afraid to touch her, although that was all he had wanted for so many months, to be back with her and pick up their life together where they'd left off. But he didn't know how to find his way back now. She could sense it as she looked at him, when he sat down on the couch and stretched his legs in front of him.

"Are you okay?" she asked him gently, and he nodded, but she knew he wasn't. She didn't know what part of him was broken, but something was, deep inside him. She could tell. "Do you want something to eat?" He shook his head. The words wouldn't come. They were stuck. It had happened to him before, in Afghanistan, when the going got too rough for him, and he was forced to be there anyway, and be part of it, and act as though he was okay with it.

She didn't want to ask him if he wanted to go to bed. She had a deep instinctive sense that he wasn't ready for that. The culture shock of coming back was too great, the trauma of whatever it was he'd been through. She could feel it in her bones and in her heart.

"Do you want to go for a walk?" she asked him, and he hesitated.

"Yeah, maybe." There'd been briefings about what it would be like coming home, but he hadn't been prepared for how beautiful she would be, how sweet and clean and innocent, and how normal it would all seem. But he didn't belong there anymore. He knew it even if she didn't. He didn't deserve to be there.

It was a beautiful June afternoon, and they walked to the Cloisters and through a garden she used to go to sometimes to study. Then they went back to the apartment and he lay down on the bed, and she stretched out next to him. He looked up at the ceiling and found some of the words he wanted to tell her.

"It's harder coming back than I thought it would be. Everything seems so normal." It seemed like a benign statement, but it was very profound. "I don't feel normal yet." He wondered if he ever would again.

"You will. Give it time. You just got here," she said softly. "We have our whole lives ahead of us. And you don't ever have to go back there." She was glad they were going to Newport. She thought it would do him good to go back to the places he had loved in his childhood, where everything was simple, despite the grand houses. They could do simple things there.

They lay next to each other and held hands until he fell asleep. For months he had dreamed of making love to her, and now he couldn't. He didn't want to. He didn't want to soil her with the things he'd seen, as though they would rub off on her.

He slept for hours because of the time difference for him, while she moved around the apartment silently, packing to go to Newport. She packed for him too. He woke up at midnight and he was ravenous. He ate nearly everything she had in the fridge, and she cooked a steak she had bought for him. She was happy to see him eat it. He needed to put back on the weight he'd lost. He looked like a skeleton.

He took a shower after he ate, and she walked into the bathroom and took her clothes off and joined him. She made it all so simple, as she stood in the water with him, looking even more beautiful than he had remembered her, and he started to cry, and suddenly his arms were around her and they were making love, and they went back to her bed and made love there, and he found her again. He thought he had lost her, and himself. He was still crying when he

Joy

came, and then the tears stopped, and he was at peace as he lay next to her.

"Welcome back," she said, still breathless from their lovemaking.

"I'm never leaving you again," he whispered, and meant it at that moment.

"You don't have to. I'm here, Shep. I'm not going anywhere."

"I'm sorry I had to leave you to go to Afghanistan."

"It's over now, like a bad dream." She couldn't even imagine how bad it had been. But he looked like he was waking up. They lay together and talked about nothing important, just ordinary things, until they fell asleep. It was what he needed now. She always knew what he needed. He was part of her heart and soul, as she was of his. He had a nightmare that night, but it didn't wake him up. She held him in her arms until he relaxed and fell into a deep sleep again. As the sun came up, she fell asleep next to him, grateful beyond words that he was home.

The drive to Newport was more beautiful than either of them remembered. It was perfect. He had called his parents to tell them he was home and would see them in a few days, and they had given him permission to use their house. Unlike the VanderHolts, they didn't have employees who lived there year-round. They brought people from Boston with them when they came down, and the house was empty the rest of the time. Shep and Allegra could be there alone now, which was what they needed. She didn't want to stay at her grandmother's home with all the staff there. This was what he needed. His boyhood home would be an easier reentry for him.

They swam off his parents' dock when they got there, and went for a walk. They went to the store and bought groceries. They bought lobsters for dinner and Shep cooked them, and they sat outside and looked at the stars afterward. Then they made love again as they had the night before, but it was easy and familiar this time. He had gotten stronger and looked healthier even in a few days. He had shaved off his mustache and looked like himself again.

Shep went to Boston alone to see his parents, and Allegra visited her grandmother's cottage while he was away for the day. The staff were happy to see her, and she had come to love her grandmother's beautiful home, even though she had been unhappy there as a child and had felt unwelcome. She was welcome there as an adult, now that her grandmother understood who she was, and that she was nothing like her mother.

Allegra lay reading on a chair in the garden all afternoon, and Shep came to get her when he got back from Boston. He was always impressed when he visited her grandparents' cottage. It was one of the biggest and most imposing homes in Newport. a throwback to another era of grander lives and greater riches. The VanderHolts had held on to it through generations. The Williamses had acquired their home more recently. Shep's grandparents had bought it.

They drove back to his house and swam off the dock again, and made love in his bedroom afterward. She loved knowing that it had been his room as a boy, and now she was his wife.

"How were your parents?" she asked him, as they made dinner and ate in the big old-fashioned kitchen.

"Old. They've aged a lot just in the last six months. I worry about them. My brothers should come to see them more often. We had a

Joy

nice visit," he said, looking peaceful. Just the two days he'd been home had begun to restore him and heal the wounds of everything he'd been through. He needed a lot more of it.

They spent two weeks there, which did him a world of good, and then they went back to New York. She had interviews with the two publishers she'd heard from. They were going to take turns commuting to Washington on weekends. They were just starting out on their grown-up lives. His parents wanted him to come back to Boston in a year, when he left the military, but he and Allegra wanted to live in New York. It was more exciting. He was looking forward to weekends there.

He'd been home for three weeks and it was the end of June when they went to Washington so he could report to the intelligence office. He seemed almost like his old self again. He was getting there, and had only had one nightmare in the last week, which was a vast improvement over one or more per night when he first got home. He'd gained some weight, and looked more like the Shep she knew. When they went to Washington, they checked in to their favorite inn in Georgetown. It was quaint and cozy and they loved it. She did some shopping when he went to take care of his paperwork, and he had made reservations that night at 1789, their favorite restaurant, to celebrate his homecoming. He had served for four years and had done a tour of duty in Afghanistan and survived it. He couldn't wait for the next year to go by, so he could leave the army and embrace civilian life. He had all the tools he needed to find a good job, after five years in Army Intelligence by the time they released him.

He was quiet when he got back from the office, she noticed that he still tired easily, and he was withdrawn until dinner that night.

She wondered if it had been traumatic going back to the intelligence office. He didn't say anything to her until they were eating dinner. She could see he had something to tell her before he said it.

"So, are you settled in at work?" she asked him, smiling, and he hesitated. He waited too long to answer her, and he looked serious when he did.

"They made me an offer. For extra pay," he said quietly.

"Doing what?" she asked, suspicious.

There was no way around it, except to tell her. "They want me to go back to Afghanistan for another six-month tour of duty, and then finish up in Washington when I get back. I'll go back as captain, better base salary and combat pay. They need me there, Allie." He hadn't called her that since she was a teenager.

"My father is still there," she said bleakly. "That's never a good sign. He only goes to the worst places."

"They really do need me, Allegra. We can save the money. They swore I'd be home for Christmas."

"And when would you leave?" She felt sick as she listened to him, and she could tell they had convinced him. He wanted to go. She could see it in his eyes. They had won. They had their hooks in him now.

"In two weeks. They would let me come home early, a few days before Christmas." His voice was a low growl. "And I'll do six months in Washington after the holidays, and then I'm done."

"Is this what it's going to be? They talk you into going back every time, and one day you wind up like my father? A robot. Three weeks ago you were having nightmares, and you looked broken when you came home."

Joy

"I'll have a desk job and work on strategy and statistics this time. No field work. No interrogations. No torture."

"Isn't that what they told you last time? Maybe this is how they roped my father in, except there was a real war on in Vietnam then. Maybe that life becomes addictive. But you can't bounce back every time. One day there will be nothing left of you and you'll be broken forever, like he is."

"I'm not at that point yet. And we're talking another six months in Afghanistan, not forever. I can do it. And I make a difference for my country there. Six months till Christmas is a short tour of duty, it's not like a year or two years."

"If you survive it, body and mind." He had ruined the evening for her, and the celebration of his homecoming was over in three short weeks. He was going back, and she knew there was nothing she could do to stop him. They had hooked him, and he was ready to go back to a god-awful place, and they would send him back to her broken. "Do I have a choice?" she asked, looking upset.

"Maybe not so much," he said honestly. "I feel like I should do it. I owe the army a lot. I told them I had to talk to you about it. I didn't agree to anything yet." She nodded and was grateful for that.

"You have to do what you think is right, Shep. But I wish you wouldn't go. You got back relatively whole, next time maybe you won't." He had recovered in a few weeks this time but he had been in bad shape mentally when he got home.

"I swear I can handle another six months, and it's a better job this time, with a higher rank."

"Then I guess you'll go," she said sadly, and he smiled ruefully and thanked her. He had already forgotten how much he hated Afghanistan. They had promised him it would be better this time, and he believed them.

She was sad as they walked back to the inn after dinner. She loved having him home, and now he was going again. He felt guilty for upsetting her, but he was convinced it was the right thing to do. They knew just how to do it. "Where do you want to spend the next two weeks before you go?" she asked him.

"How about a week in Newport, and a week in New York afterward?" Their time together already had the bittersweet taste of goodbye to it. She hated the idea of his being back in a war zone. She just didn't want him to turn into her father, but she didn't see how he could, Shep was such a decent, warm, loving man. Her father was a war machine who had sold his soul years before, and there was no turning back from that. He never had. She wanted to believe that Shep could survive another six-month tour of duty in Afghanistan and remain whole. Maybe it wouldn't affect him so much this time. He knew what to expect. She could only hope.

The two weeks flew by. They spent a week in Newport, at his parents' home, as he wanted to. They had dinner with his parents in Boston before they headed back to New York. They were surprised to see her with him. Shep and Allegra had thought about telling them they were married, but decided against it. It would just give his parents one more thing to worry about. His going back to Afghanistan was enough. They were upset about it, and so was Allegra, but he had made the decision to go for six more months. She didn't tell her grandmother about their marriage either. The time

JOY

was wrong for her too. She had lost her husband three months before and was still in deep mourning. She didn't need to hear about Shep going to Afghanistan.

The week Allegra and Shep spent together in New York was almost perfect, except that his leaving again was looming, and Allegra never forgot it for a second. She was already sad before he left. He promised her this would be the last time. And he wouldn't reenlist when his five years were up, after six more months in Washington. After Afghanistan, he would come to New York every weekend, as he had before, since presumably she would have a job by then. She didn't want to look for a job in Washington, when he wouldn't be there for six months and she'd be alone. And all the publishers she wanted to work for were in New York. She was going to keep the apartment near Columbia, and then move to be closer to her work. She'd have to do all of it without Shep, but the job would keep her busy, just as her studies had done.

It was a painful déjà vu when she went back to Washington with him, and she resented the army for talking him into it. But he was upbeat and optimistic, and convinced he was doing the right thing for his country, giving the army another six months in a combat zone. At twenty-six, he felt up to it, and ready to take whatever job they were assigning him to, which he couldn't disclose to her. Clearly he liked it. And he was going back as a captain, which he was happy about too. He didn't have a single nightmare the week before he left. Officially he had recovered from his last tour there. At least it seemed that way. She had had him home for five short weeks and now he was going away again, for more of what he'd been through before. He was flying back to Afghanistan on the Fourth of July.

"Don't make a habit of places like that," she warned him, and he promised he wouldn't. She couldn't imagine him staying in the army either. He was ready for civilian life after four years now of active duty, with one more year to go.

The last time they made love before he left had the same bittersweet quality as his last days with her. She felt as though Shep belonged to the military now, and had only been on loan to her when he came home. She had lived that life with her father, and she didn't want it for Shep or herself.

He kissed her hard when they said goodbye. "Don't forget me!" There was desperation in his voice.

"Not likely," she said. There were tears in her eyes, but he didn't look as torn this time. He hadn't just been assigned to go, he had chosen to accept the job, which made a difference to him. He had a voice in it. "Take care of yourself," she said, and kissed him one last time. "I love you."

"I love you too," he said, and left her. He turned back with a final wave, as she fervently hoped that this would be the last time he would leave her to go to another war zone. At least he would be home by Christmas. She had spent the previous one alone. She didn't want to do that again.

Chapter 5

Allegra heard from Shep when he got to Kandahar. She thought about him constantly and felt like the bottom had dropped out of her world again. She checked in with her grandmother, knowing that she was still sad about her husband's death. Mariette was planning to spend the summer in Newport, although she was sad to be there without him, but she wanted to follow their traditions, and didn't want to spend the summer in New York. She invited her granddaughter to join her. Allegra had had several more job interviews, but no one had made her an offer yet. She was managing financially on the allowance her father gave her every month. She wasn't extravagant, but it was just enough for her to pay her rent and eat and for additional minor necessities, without frills or luxuries. She budgeted carefully. And Shep's army pay helped her too. His promotion to captain made a difference. But she still needed a job and wanted her own salary. She didn't want to be dependent on her husband and father.

She accepted her grandmother's invitation as a kindness to her, in return for all the holidays they had allowed her to stay with them. It seemed like the least she could do. Mariette hadn't heard from Isabelle since the funeral, which didn't surprise Allegra.

There were lapses between calls from Shep, and when Allegra heard from him, he sounded exhausted, and different from the last time he was there. He didn't sound as shell-shocked as he had then. He had a better idea of what to expect in a combat zone in that part of the world. She thought he sounded hardened at times, and cynical. There had been a loss of innocence since he had gone to war. He had seen things that ordinary people in the States never would. She didn't want his time there to ruin him or break him. It was a constant worry every moment he was away. He was tender and loving when he spoke to her and wrote to her, but between the lines, she could sense something different in him, something harder, which worried her.

Newport wasn't the same without him. She was as lonely as she had been there in her childhood, with no one to talk to now except her grandmother. Mariette wasn't in the mood for company. She had to be encouraged to get up and dress and eat, none of which she wanted to do. She declined all of her friends' invitations and turned down their offers to visit. Allegra coaxed her to take walks in the garden, sit in the sun, and do errands in town with her. She used every excuse to keep her moving and get her out of her room. Mariette's health seemed to be faltering. Allegra could see that she had lost her will to live, and discussed it with her grandmother's doctor

Joy

when he came to check on her. None of it surprised him. It was typical of most people who lost a spouse of fifty years. The challenge would be for her to find a reason to go on living without him. All of Allegra's efforts were helpful and kept Mariette going through the summer. She and Arthur had enjoyed their social life in Newport. They were out almost every night, and now she never wanted to leave the house or see any of their friends. She took a tray in her room whenever possible, instead of eating in the dining room with Allegra.

"People are going to think I'm very poor company if you don't eat with me occasionally, Grandmother," she said, trying to tease her out of it, but she didn't get far. Mariette was suffering from lethargy and a lack of interest in the world, as the result of her grief. She had no idea of the strain Allegra was under, constantly waiting to hear from Shep, and praying that he wouldn't get hurt or killed in Afghanistan.

Since she hadn't found a job yet, she was able to stay with Mariette until the end of August. She went back to New York after Labor Day to pursue the search more energetically. Mariette decided to stay in Newport through September. The season was over by then. Most of her friends had gone back to Boston or New York or Washington, which was where the summer residents came from. So she had fewer people to avoid, and hardly got out of bed after Allegra left. Allegra called frequently to check on her, and the reports from the housekeeper weren't encouraging. Allegra felt sorry for her grandmother but couldn't do much from a distance. Mariette didn't want to talk on the phone either.

Two weeks after Labor Day, Allegra's calls to the employment agencies finally started to produce some results. She was sent on interviews at three different publishing houses. One of them asked her back for a second interview, which was a hopeful sign. It was a big, very respected publisher, and they had an opening for an editorial assistant.

Her school record was excellent, and a diploma from Columbia was a strong point in her favor. She got the job for a shockingly low salary, but she thought she could manage on it if she was very careful, and Shep would be out of the army in nine months, in June, and presumably earning more than he made in the military. She was grateful to get an entry-level job at an important publishing house. Her years of reading everything she could lay hands on would pay off now. She was extremely well read, which the interviewers had questioned her about. She had read some very obscure books, which impressed them.

She would be taught how to work on the manuscripts of previously unpublished, unknown authors, and learn how to get their books edited and ready for publication. It sounded exciting to Allegra, and she was thrilled to get the job. She had a week before her start date to find a new apartment. The publisher was in the West Forties, and she found a fifth-floor walkup in an old but well-kept building in Hell's Kitchen, which was becoming gentrified and was close enough for her to walk to work, saving her some money. She didn't mind the endless stairs. That had eliminated older tenants from wanting the apartment. It faced south, and was sunny. It had been freshly painted white. It was tiny, but big enough for her and Shep. Her father's allowance, added to her modest salary and Shep's army pay, would help her cover the rent. Bradley was still sending her money, since he didn't know she had married Shep. She knew it

Joy

was dishonest of her not to tell him, but she needed the help, and once Shep came home and found a civilian job, she would tell him.

She had to hire a moving company to bring her furniture to the new apartment and get it up the five flights of stairs. She got rid of a few things that were too battered by then, but she kept the rest, so she didn't have to spend much money on the apartment. She had enough to furnish it. She did everything she could herself. She had learned to be frugal as a student, not wanting to be a burden on anyone. Her grandmother gave her checks occasionally for her birthday and Christmas, and she saved them for when she needed something she couldn't afford otherwise. She upgraded some of the furniture with it. She wanted the apartment to be pretty when Shep came home.

By the end of September, she had a job and a new home. It was a major leap into adulthood, and she was excited to go to work every day.

Her grandmother came home from Newport two weeks after she'd started her new job, and Allegra went to visit her on a Saturday. She was shocked to see that Mariette had lost a considerable amount of weight in the month Allegra hadn't been with her. Clearly no one was urging her to eat, and they were letting her waste away. Allegra stayed until lunchtime on her visit, and told her grandmother all about her new job, as she encouraged Mariette to eat a few mouthfuls of what had been sent up on a tray to her bedroom.

"You have to do better than that, Grandmother," Allegra said gently.

"Why? I don't go out anymore. With Arthur gone, I don't want to go out or see anyone. So what difference does it make if I eat?"

"That's not right. Grandfather wouldn't like that. You have to stay strong."

"Why? I never see Isabelle. I don't want to go to dinner parties alone. And you're sweet to visit me, but you have your own life to lead. I don't recall seeing Shepherd Williams this summer. Have you had a falling-out and stopped seeing him?" It was the first time Mariette had asked about him, and Allegra was touched. It had taken her three months to notice his absence.

"He's still in the army. He's in Afghanistan again. He'll be back for Christmas."

"I thought I hadn't seen him around. Usually, you two are inseparable. You must miss him," Mariette said. The way she said it brought tears to Allegra's eyes, which she didn't want her grandmother to see. She didn't want her to know how much she missed Shep, or how worried she was about him.

"I do miss him," she said quietly, and continued to try and get her grandmother to eat a little more of the food. The curtains were drawn and the room was dark, although it was a beautiful sunny day outside. She tried to interest Mariette in a walk, but she didn't want to get out of bed. She hadn't gone for a walk outdoors since Allegra left Newport over a month before.

Allegra was sad when she left her. There was so little she could do. She went back to her apartment, put together a bookcase she'd bought, and shelved her books. She didn't mind the tiny size of the apartment. It was flooded with sunlight, and the furniture was comfortable and familiar. She couldn't wait for Shep to see it. Christmas didn't seem so far away now. He was halfway through his tour.

Her job kept her busy. She brought manuscripts home on most

Joy

nights, evaluating them and using the skills she was learning to do light editing. She worked until late every night. Some of the manuscripts were very good, others less so. Reading them was inspiring, and made her think of writing one day. But she was a long way from there. She was twenty-two years old, in her first job, and still learning how to be an editor.

She wrote Shep about her job, and he told her how much he missed her. By November, she was already planning what they would do on Christmas when he got home. All he had to do then was commute from Washington on weekends for six months, and then they'd be like any other couple, working at their jobs and living together. The idea of a wedding reception seemed silly to her now. They were already married. She felt like she had belonged to him forever, and a wedding now with West Point cadets in dress uniforms seemed absurd. She just wanted Shep to come home in one piece. That was the only thing she needed.

Her grandmother didn't celebrate Thanksgiving that year. She had no desire to celebrate it without Arthur. Allegra went to see her in the morning, and she was still asleep. Allegra realized Mariette was going to spend the day in bed, so she went back to her apartment alone. Shepherd called her that night, and they had a few minutes to talk. He said he was going out on a mission and had just enough time to tell her he loved her before he hung up. He had told her before he left that there would be no missions in the field this time, which apparently wasn't true.

She spent the rest of the weekend editing and got a lot of work done. The senior editor she worked for was always impressed by how hard Allegra worked and how much she accomplished. It was easy for her. She had no other life than her job. She was friendly with the other women who worked there. There were a few other editorial assistants, all of them older than she was, and she liked them, but most of the time she kept to herself. She was very private about her personal life, and professional in the office. She wore her wedding ring and they knew she was married, but she never talked about Shep or said he was in Afghanistan. She shared no personal details at work and was very serious about her job. She was quiet and dignified, and mature for her age. Her senior editor thought she was unusual and gave a glowing report of Allegra to her superiors.

It seemed like Shep had been gone a lifetime when the day finally came for him to come home. Allegra had already done her Christmas shopping for him. She had bought him two sweaters to wear on weekends when he was out of uniform, and a watch with her Christmas bonus. She took the train to Washington the night before he was due home. He had already told her he had six weeks off, after combat duty.

It seemed like a miracle that he was coming home uninjured. He'd been lucky, and so was she that no harm had come to him. She smiled nearly all the way to Washington on the train and checked in to another familiar hotel near the base. They had a brightly lit Christmas tree in the lobby and Christmas decorations up.

Allegra had bought a small tree for the apartment and decorated it. His presents were wrapped and under the tree. But the best gift of all was Shep. She could hardly wait to see him and couldn't sleep that night. She was up at six, knowing he was due to land at ten and

Joy

could leave the base immediately. There would be a physical thirty days later, but no procedures until then.

She went to the base at eleven, to give him time to get organized to leave. She had just gotten to the visiting area when she saw him walk in, in his uniform, with a duffel bag over his shoulder. His face broke into a broad grin when he saw her, and they collided as she ran toward him and threw herself into his arms. He held her tight and kissed her. He didn't have a mustache this time, but she could feel that he had lost a lot of weight again. He took a step back, the better to see her, and she could see an intense look in his eyes. There was nothing she could define clearly, other than the weight, but he looked different. He couldn't wait to leave the base with her.

They took a cab to the car rental agency. He wanted to drive this time. He got behind the wheel, for the long drive to New York, and kissed her again.

"I told you I'd be home for Christmas," he said triumphantly. He couldn't wait to have six weeks off with her, to settle into their relationship and routine before he had to report back for duty in Washington.

They never stopped talking all the way back to New York. She told him more about her job, and he told her all the things he wanted to do. He said nothing about Afghanistan, just as he hadn't before. It was the nature of his assignment in intelligence. He had a high security clearance, but he had other things to say to her, and whenever possible, he leaned over and kissed her.

He asked about her grandmother, and Allegra said she wasn't doing well. She rarely left her bed anymore. She wasn't that old, but the spirit had gone out of her when she lost her husband.

"I think that happens a lot with people who've been married for a very long time. I'm sorry to hear it," Shep said.

They got to New York at six o'clock. The stores were decorated for the holiday, they could see Christmas trees in every window, and he looked around their new neighborhood with interest.

"It seems a little rough around the edges," he commented as he looked at the older buildings, and a few remaining tenements.

"It's improving. They're gentrifying the area. I was lucky to get the apartment I did. The rents in the renovated buildings are much higher. Our building is old, but it's well taken care of and clean."

They hurried up the stairs together and as soon as he closed the door behind him, he pulled Allegra into his arms and kissed her. He could see the bedroom from the door, and headed straight there with her in his arms and set her down on the bed, and within seconds their clothes were off and they were swept away on a wave of passion that had been building for six months, and nothing had changed. He was still the man she knew and loved and had grown up with. She was enormously relieved to see that Afghanistan hadn't ruined him, or affected him the way it had before. They'd been lucky.

After they made love, she handed him his old bathrobe, and he wandered into the living room, sat down, and looked around. He recognized the old furniture in the room, liked the new pieces, and saw what a nice job she'd done arranging everything.

"Whose Christmas presents?" he asked with a boyish grin, and she laughed.

"Who do you think? Santa Claus left them for you."

Joy

"I have to go shopping. I didn't bring anything back from Kandahar for you. There's nothing you'd want there. It's a mess right now. And we're not helping. The whole place is a war zone. I'm glad they let me come home. I was worried they wouldn't."

She came to sit next to him and nestled close. He put an arm around her and held her, and he was quiet as he looked at the lights on the tree. There was a faraway look in his eyes that she'd noticed before, in the car. He had obviously brought his memories back. She knew he'd share them when he was ready, to the degree he could. So much of what he did he couldn't tell her. She had told him all about her job in the car on the ride home, and he had slept for a while when she drove.

Shep kept looking around the apartment as though it was a palace and he couldn't believe he was there.

"They sent us to one of the provinces on our last assignment. We were living in shacks and mud huts. You have no idea what this looks like to me now. Everything is beautiful, and so are you." He traced her features with his finger and it drifted down her neck to her breast, and he kissed her, the passion mounting in both of them. They were starving for each other. After they made love again, she poured him a glass of wine, while she made dinner. She'd bought him a steak because he loved them. She noticed as he held his glass of wine that his hand was shaking, enough so that she spotted it easily. She didn't want to ask him about it on their first night together. But it concerned her. And when she looked into his eyes, she saw the same pain she'd seen when he came back last time. Afghanistan had left its mark on him again. There was no way to come back from places like that unscathed. The signs were just more subtle this time, and over dinner she saw that he didn't smile the way he used to. He looked like he had the weight of the world on his heart. She realized that he had just gotten better at hiding it than he had been the first time.

He slept soundly that night and was up at five because of the time difference. He woke her to make love to her. She had taken the day off. It was Friday, and she'd taken the day before as well, to meet him in Washington. It was the weekend before Christmas, which was on the coming Wednesday. Just as they'd promised him, he was home for Christmas. She had to work on Monday and half a day on Tuesday, and then she had the rest of the week off to spend with him. He was planning to go to Boston for the day on Monday to see his parents. But he wanted to spend time with her first on the weekend. They were going to spend the holiday together, alone in the apartment.

After they made love, they went back to sleep, woke up late, and she made him a big breakfast of pancakes and eggs and bacon. He devoured it and once again, she noticed his hands shaking and wondered if he'd been sick in Kandahar and hadn't told her. He saw her notice, as he set his fork down, and he shrugged.

"Occupational hazard," he said lightly. "It's nothing."

"Did you tell a doctor over there?" she asked, worried.

"They've seen it before, in combat zones."

"Were you in the combat zones a lot?" she asked gently. He'd never told her. It was supposed to be an office job this time, but she knew it wasn't.

"Enough, but never for long. We went on specific missions and came back pretty fast. The enlisted guys have to stick around. MI doesn't. We're there for a reason, or to assess an area." It was the most he had ever told her about it.

"It must be stressful as hell," she said, thinking of his shaking hands.

"That's what we're there for." He smiled, and for a second he looked like a stranger. There was a look in his eyes as if he was someone who had joined a cult and was proud to be part of it. That look hadn't been there last time. The combat zone had come home with him.

They went for a long walk and admired the Christmas windows. It was a luxury to have a day off to spend with him. While they walked, he said something about his brothers.

"You'll have to meet them one of these days, when we tell them all we're married. Do we still want a wedding?" he asked her. It felt strange to be back in a normal world of Christmas decorations and weddings. It was hard to get used to, but he knew he had to.

"I don't know," she said about a wedding. "My grandmother would have to give it, and she's in no condition to. My father's in Afghanistan, and he wouldn't know what to do, and probably doesn't care. And we can use the money for other things. So maybe not." She looked mildly disappointed, but the thrill of having him home eclipsed and outweighed a lost chance to have a wedding. "It doesn't really matter. We have us." He nodded, relieved they didn't have to go through it.

"I guess we have to tell them," he said. "They're going to say you're too young. I'm not, but you are." She felt a lot older than twenty-two now. She felt as though she had lived several lifetimes.

"It's kind of fun keeping it a secret. We don't have to deal with anyone's opinions. Maybe I'll tell my father the next time he comes home. Did you tell the army?" she asked him.

He nodded. "I had to, so you get widow's benefits if I die," he said matter-of-factly. "But I marked it confidential." That sounded reasonable to her. He didn't seem like a boy to her anymore. He was a man now. He would be turning twenty-seven soon, but he looked much older. Whatever he had seen in Afghanistan had not only matured him, it had aged him. It was an ugly war. They all were. But Afghanistan was particularly so and had broken and disillusioned many men before him. She could see the disappointment in his eyes, and the sadness.

They went to see the tree at Rockefeller Center and went ice-skating, the way they had when they were kids. Now they were married, which made Allegra feel very grown-up, especially when Shep was home. Their marriage seemed more real when he was with her. There was a dreamlike quality to it when she was alone.

She noticed that he didn't speak about the future the way he used to. He wasn't talking about finding a job in June, or what direction his civilian career should take. He seemed more fatalistic after living with the risk of death every day. He was more cynical. He had been so innocent when he was younger, and so hopeful about life. Now he was less so. He had seen what ugly detours it could take, into unexpected danger zones. He had watched men die in front of him, both the enemy and his comrades. He had seen death meted out, and unexpected deaths that arrived swiftly and never should have occurred.

"No war should ever happen," he told her. "It destroys too many men." She was grateful it hadn't destroyed him, and that he had

Joy

come back to her in one piece, even if his hands shook. She assumed that that would go away eventually. He was young and had survived.

They had a late lunch at a delicatessen after they went skating, and then they walked home. It was cold, but the air felt good on their faces as they walked through the theater district on the way to Hell's Kitchen. The usual familiar musicals were playing and so was a new production of *A Christmas Carol*. She had loved *The Nutcracker* as a child. Grandmother Dixon had taken her to see it once, in a rare burst of holiday generosity, and Allegra had never forgotten it. It was her only happy memory of them.

They settled into the apartment as it began to snow outside.

"It looks like it's going to be a white Christmas," she said, as they sat down on the couch, and he looked angry for a minute.

"Fuck Christmas." He said it vehemently and startled her, it was unlike him. "Do you realize how many men died in Afghanistan this year?" He spoke so harshly that she was shocked for a minute and didn't know what to say. He had always loved Christmas.

"I'm sorry. I didn't mean to offend you. I'm sure I don't know enough about the war there. But you never tell me about it," she said gently.

"I can't. What I know is classified, and some of it is top secret. But trust me, it's ugly." She could tell from the way he looked, and from what he had just said. It was dark, and they'd been out all day. She could tell that he was tired. He'd only been home for two days. He was still adjusting to normal life back in the States.

"Do you think you should get some counseling?" she asked him cautiously while they ate dinner. The last time he came home he had been sad and broken. This time he was angry, she could feel it bubbling under the surface. It seemed like a powerful force that he was trying to restrain.

"I don't need counseling, I'm fine," he said brusquely, and brushed off the suggestion. "I'm happy to be home." She didn't want to tell him he seemed angry to her, she didn't want to hurt his feelings. She saw nothing shameful in talking to a therapist, but he did, so she didn't bring it up again.

After he went to Boston to see his parents, he said that it went well, but he offered no details. Allegra had known his parents for years. They always seemed very cool and disengaged to her, and Shep always said he wasn't close to them. He very rarely mentioned his brothers, or even his parents, except to say that they were closer to his brothers and had never understood him. She didn't press him about it, since he only said it when he was drunk, which didn't happen often.

The day after he'd been to Boston, on Christmas Eve, he had a nightmare, and she awoke to hear him crying in his sleep. He was shouting something about a land mine, and then he was sobbing. She couldn't wake him when she tried. He was in a profound sleep. She held him and he finally calmed down and didn't stir again. But she lay awake for a long time, watching him and worrying about him. He was subtly different from when he left, but the difference was enough to concern her, and she wondered what part of him they had broken this time. Whatever it was, it was buried deep.

Chapter 6

Shep and Allegra went to drop a gift off for her grandmother on Christmas Eve. The housekeeper told them she was sleeping and wasn't feeling well, so they left the gift with her. Allegra sensed that Mariette was wasting away, grieving for her husband, and choosing not to return to the land of the living herself.

They spent Christmas alone in the apartment, and Shep loved his gifts from her. The sweaters fit perfectly, and he put the watch on immediately. He had bought Allegra a sweater in a soft green, the color of her eyes, and a narrow gold bracelet that she loved too. It had a little gold heart dangling from it, and he'd had the date engraved on the back. It was their second married Christmas, their first one together. The first one he'd spent in Afghanistan, as well as their first anniversary.

They had a quiet day together, watched old movies on TV, and ate popcorn. It was snowing again, and a perfect day to be at home, tucked into bed, and making love. They were living in their own private world.

Shep waited until the first week of January, after the holidays, to tell Allegra that he had made a decision. She could tell that it was something important. His hands were shaking, as they did most of the time now, when he told her. She wanted him to see a doctor, and he said he'd see one on the base when he went back to Washington. He still insisted it was nothing. She wasn't convinced. Sometimes she could feel his whole body shivering when he was asleep, as though he was ice cold. He didn't have the same nightmares this time, but frequently he either cried or shouted in his sleep. Afghanistan had left its mark on him again. More than she knew. He shared his decision with her on a Sunday morning.

"I'm going to stay with the army," he said. "I'm going to reenlist when my time is up. I like the work I do. It's a good job, and I think it's the right career for me." He looked determined, even belligerent, and she felt her heart pound as he said it. It was the last thing she wanted. The army had ruined her father. She didn't want it to ruin Shep. He wasn't the same kind of man. She didn't want to be married to a man like her father, one who was never at home and always on the other side of the world somewhere. That wasn't what she had signed on for. He had promised her he'd get out. Now he'd changed his mind. He was a tender person, a gentle soul. The army would destroy him.

"What does that mean for us?" Allegra asked him in a choked voice.

"I can wind up in a desk job in Washington eventually, doing interesting work I love. I won't be sent to places like Afghanistan all the time. This is just the beginning. After this, it will settle down."

Joy

"And if it doesn't?"

"I can request posts in the States."

"And they can send you wherever they want, if they say they need you there." She knew how it worked. She had lived it all her life with her father, although he was an extreme case, and he wanted to be sent to war zones. That was his specialty, and his strong suit. It wasn't Shep's. His two tours of duty in Afghanistan had taken a toll on him.

"I'd like to try it as a career. If it doesn't work out, I don't have to reenlist again, and I can get interesting jobs after this, in international security work, industrial espionage, positions that use my strategic skills."

"There are no war zones in civilian life, Shep. You don't have to go around killing and torturing people in a regular job. And once you head down that path, there's no turning back. Look at my father and what it turned him into. He's a killing machine. That's not who you are. The only people who come back from it come back broken or severely damaged. Take a look at your hands, that's how it starts." She spoke to him in a calm clear voice. "My father's father was just like him, maybe worse. It runs in my family. You wanted a career in business. That would be a lot better for you, and for us."

"I've developed skills that I can use in the army better than anywhere else. I'm someone in the army. I'll be nothing in civilian life."

"One of these times, if you go back to places like Afghanistan, it will break you. It already is."

"It's stressful, but I can handle it," he assured her. She didn't believe him, but she knew she couldn't change his mind. They had hooked him. They owned him now. It was what they did so well. A secret club you could never escape from once you'd been initiated. And clearly he had been. He was a member in good standing now.

"What deal have you already made with them?" she asked. When she looked him in the eye, she could tell he already knew. She wondered if he knew when he came home and didn't want to tell her until after the holidays. He squirmed when she asked him. He was guilty as charged.

"I want to re-up and see how far I can go. I'd like to achieve a high rank before I leave the military." He was already a captain. "I have to be back in Washington on the eighth of February. They want to send me back to Afghanistan on March first. I'd come home for Christmas again, and then I'd do a six-month tour at the Pentagon, before they send me away again." He was leaving for another ten months. "Whenever I leave the military, I'll have had an incredible amount of experience before I'm thirty. You won't even be twenty-six yet. We're still young. We can start a family then if you want, and I'll be sure I stick around, and stay in Washington as much as I can. I want to stay in till I'm thirty." Another four years of Russian roulette.

"You can never be sure they'll leave you in Washington. If they told you that, they lied. They'll send you wherever they want you, no matter what they promise you now. You've been home for two weeks, and you want to go back to Afghanistan for ten months." She had lost him to the army, and she knew it. No matter how long they stretched it out, he was already theirs. Their poison was in his veins. That's why he was shaking and shouting at night. And what was left of who he used to be cried in his sleep. It seemed tragic to her. The waste of a wonderful human being. The worst part was that she loved him and didn't want to leave him. "What am I left with? You come home every year for Christmas, like the Ghost of Christmas Past? A little more broken each time until one day you can't fix it anymore. The only things left are the broken parts. You're throwing your life away." And hers, she thought but didn't say.

"Don't be so dramatic. I'm stronger than you think. I can hold up to it."

"No one can," she said sadly. "Look how many men it breaks. Sooner or later it will break you."

"The ones who break are the weak ones," he said firmly. She shook her head.

"No, those are the ones who tried to hang on to what was left of them. They'll own you, Shep, and do whatever they want with you. And when you're too damaged to be of use to them, they'll throw you away, or park you in some shit job you'll hate. They revere men like my father, who'll do anything. That isn't you."

He wanted to play in the big leagues, but he had no idea what it would cost him. "And I don't want to have kids one day with a man who's never here. I grew up that way. I won't do that to someone else."

"We're not ready to have kids yet. We can talk about it when we are." She could see that there was no talking him out of it. He had made up his mind. They won. They had him now, with the tantalizing offer of exciting jobs.

What he told her cast a pall on the rest of his time with her in New York. She went to work and came home to him at night. What he planned to do, making the army his career, stood between them like a boulder. The tone of his visit changed after that. It was just a visit, not a life.

He went back to Washington at the beginning of February, and came home for two weekends after that. He was going back to Afghanistan on March first. She wasn't going to see him off this time. She couldn't bear to see it and dreaded who he would be when he came back.

By sheer coincidence, her father came to the States for a week in February. He came to see Allegra in New York for a day. She tried to talk to him about it, how Shep was the wrong man for them to turn into one of their killing machines, a star strategist who would see all the horrors of the war.

"It'll destroy him," she said over lunch.

"He's tougher than that. He's already been put to some hard tests, and passed with flying colors. It's what he wants. Every wife and mother in the world would say what you just said to me. It won't kill him, Allegra. It'll make a man of him." He was never going to help her dissuade Shep.

The last weekend together was an agony for both of them. Shep felt guilty and Allegra was heartbroken. It was a poor combination, and this time she cried more after he left than when he was leaving. She didn't go to Washington with him to see him off. She went to work instead. She planned to drown herself in work for the next ten months. His leaving was good for her job, but not for her heart or her soul or her life. She was sure he was doing the wrong thing for both of them, staying in the army.

Joy

* * *

She worked hard at her job for the next ten months. She did well, and was promoted to full editor at twenty-three.

She heard from Shep and feared for his life and his soul every day. She could already hear subtle changes in him. She couldn't put her finger on what was different, but she knew he was. After the U.S. invaded Iraq in March, he was transferred there in April, to Baghdad. She turned twenty-three once he was there.

Life didn't stop because he was in Iraq. It was a loss of innocence for both of them.

In April, almost a year to the day after her husband died, Allegra's grandmother had a massive heart attack and died in her sleep. She had been willing herself to die for a year. She had given up on life when he left.

Isabelle didn't come home this time. Mariette's attorney called Isabelle to notify her, and she said she couldn't get back in time for the funeral. She was on a cruise around the world on a yacht she and her husband had chartered, and she said it was too difficult to get back.

Allegra made all the arrangements, respectfully, and planned a dignified funeral for a woman who had been kind to her in the end, had neglected her as a child but done the best she was capable of, which Allegra recognized and understood. She had learned a lot about people's inability to love in her short lifetime. She knew that Isabelle would show up eventually, at her own convenience, to settle the estate.

Mariette left Allegra a small but respectable amount of money, which would give her some comfort and enable her to do some things she wanted, without changing her life dramatically. Mariette left the bulk of her estate to her only daughter, Isabelle, according to her husband's wishes, although she hadn't entirely agreed. But she had followed his request.

In June, Allegra had another unwelcome surprise. Her father was due to return to Washington, and was planning to retire. He had no choice. Bradley had stayed in as long as they would let him. He was about to turn sixty-eight, as a lieutenant general, a three-star general. Making a final tour of one of the key combat zones in Iraq before he left, he was shot and killed by a sniper. Allegra knew it was the way he would have preferred to die, rather than dwindling as he grew old and feeble in civilian life. He died while he was still strong and vital, at the relatively young age of sixty-seven. Allegra was contacted by a member of his staff at the Pentagon. There was no one else to tell her. When she got the call, she thought they were calling about Shep, and she couldn't breathe as she sat down to hear the bad news. It was almost a relief to discover it was her father. She hadn't seen him in four months, when she had wanted him to talk Shep out of reenlisting, and he wouldn't.

She had mixed feelings about her father's death. He had never been kind to her, never taken care of her, probably never loved her. In his own way, he was a great deal like her mother. In his case, he had fulfilled his practical responsibilities, to provide her an education and see to it that she was housed somewhere as a child by a member of her family, as long as it wasn't with him. And once she

JOY

was an adult, he paid for a modest apartment and sent her a small allowance. But he had abandoned her in every significant emotional and physical way. Nonetheless, he was still her father, and she knew she should love him, but she wasn't sure she did. She didn't feel guilty about it. It was a fact, and inevitable, given how badly he had failed her as a father. She felt numb after hearing the news, unable to feel anything. And it wasn't surprising that, since he had no other living relatives, what money he had he left to Allegra. It wasn't a large amount, but it was more than she expected. He didn't own anything. He had a small, rented apartment in Washington, D.C. Material goods weren't important to him. His career in the military was everything, it meant more than people or money. What he left Allegra gave her an additional cushion to add to what her grandmother had left her. It was a respectable amount.

The army planned his funeral, so she didn't have to do it. He was buried with the full honors due his rank as three-star lieutenant general, in Arlington Cemetery. It was a very impressive ceremony, since he was highly decorated for his service, and she was surprised by how little she felt for him. She took the train back to New York alone, since Shep was in Iraq and couldn't come. He was in the midst of some top-secret operation that required him to remain there.

With her father's death, she had no living relatives except her mother, who really didn't count, by her own choice. Isabelle had never wanted to be a mother, and hadn't been. It was an odd feeling for Allegra, knowing she had no one left in the world except Shep, whom no one even knew she was married to. They had never gotten around to telling anyone when he left. She wasn't sure it mattered now. She knew she was married to him, which was enough. There was no one left to care about her.

The house in Newport belonged to her mother now, so Allegra didn't feel comfortable going there. For the first time in a dozen years, she didn't go to Newport that summer. It wouldn't have been the same without her grandmother anyway. She stayed in New York and worked all summer, which occupied her, and distracted her from the major changes she'd had in her life in the past two months. She needed time to absorb it and process it. She went out with friends from work occasionally, but kept mainly to herself.

Isabelle finally showed up in October to settle the estate. She put the cottage in Newport on the market. She had no interest in owning it, since she was married and lived in England, and had for so many years. Her life was based there now, and a large house to maintain in the States held no appeal for her. She had hated her stuffy, boring Newport summers in her youth. It saddened Allegra to know it was being sold, she had childhood memories of the cottage, some of which were dear to her. They were the only happy family memories she had.

Isabelle spent a week in New York, making decisions about her parents' apartment, which she put on the market too, sending their furniture to auction. She kept some of the paintings, which were valuable, and sold her mother's jewelry, except for a few pieces she wanted. She called Allegra and asked her to lunch, much to Allegra's surprise. She invited her to the Plaza, where she was staying, and as always looked very pretty when Allegra met her for lunch. Allegra went more out of curiosity than any hope that some deep emotional connection would happen. She knew that wasn't possible. There was no connection to be made, and Allegra was leery of her mother. Isabelle only thought about herself. No one else mattered to her.

"My God, it's a lot of work getting rid of all that stuff," Isabelle said, as soon as she sat down. She was forty-six years old and looked ten years younger, and Allegra thought she had done something to her face since the last time she saw her. "I'm trying to sell the cottage with everything in it. It will be perfect for some nouveau riche Texan who has no idea what to do with it and wants to make a splash in Newport society." She smiled. She was selling all her family history without a qualm, and Allegra's, although Allegra had never been part of it, except as an occasional visitor. She had never been treated as a full member of the family, although she was. She was an outsider and a guest. "Which reminds me." Isabelle put a small black suede box on the table in front of Allegra. "I think she'd have wanted you to have this. She loved you, in her own chilly way. They were terrible parents, and I don't suppose they were any better as grandparents," Isabelle said blithely. "I hated them when I was younger. I don't anymore. They were just very stuffy, dull people, part of a dying breed."

Allegra opened the box cautiously, and there was a small ruby heart pin in it that she knew her grandmother had loved, and she was touched. It had been a nice gesture for her mother to give it to her, and unlike Isabelle to be generous. It wasn't very valuable, or she'd have kept it herself.

"Thank you, I love it," Allegra said, feeling emotional for a moment. And then her mother rambled on about her trip, her life in

England, another cruise she was planning, as Allegra listened to her. There were no questions about Allegra's life, no concern for her being alone in the world now. They were just two women who barely knew each other meeting for lunch. Allegra had worn her narrow wedding ring, as always, concealed by another ring. And at the end of lunch, she had the feeling that she might never see her mother again. There was no reason to. Isabelle had come to New York to get rid of her parents' possessions, not to see Allegra. She was a sidebar and nothing more in Isabelle's life. Ancient history, the result of a youthful mistake. Isabelle had given Allegra up seventeen years before and didn't want her back in her life. It would have been cruel if she had intended it to be. But she didn't. Allegra was someone she had shut out of her life, and rejected all responsibility for, but didn't mind running into from time to time when circumstances threw them together. As long as she didn't have to make any effort, or care about her.

She didn't kiss Allegra goodbye or hug her, or promise to stay in touch. She just waved, and floated away the way she always did, and she might float back again one day. Allegra hoped not. They had no connection, and never had one. Isabelle saw to that. The bridges between them were gone, Mariette and Allegra's father. Without them, they would have no reason to meet again, and Isabelle wouldn't bother. Allegra knew that about her. She went back to her office, with the ruby heart brooch in her purse. It was the only sentimental possession she owned. And the only piece of her family history she had, that and all the memories she would rather forget, of people who had left her.

Chapter 7

After Isabelle left New York, Allegra was busy at work. She was working with two new writers, a man and a woman. Both were interesting first-time authors. The male author had written a medical novel which she found fascinating. She had never met him. He was an older man, close to retirement, and did his writing on Cape Cod. They only communicated in letters. His style was a little pedantic, but his plot was excellent. She'd been assigned by her senior editor to work on his book, and help the author to tighten the writing. She was assigned to the female author's manuscript as well. It was faster-paced, more modern, and livelier, since the author was very young.

Jane March had written a thriller, which Allegra thought had definite film possibilities. Allegra told her boss, Philippa Parkinson, how much she liked it. Philippa was a longtime editor who had worked for the house for twenty-seven years. She had snow-white fashionably cut hair and lively blue eyes. She was British, and Allegra admired her. She was seasoned in the business, and had given Allegra helpful pointers since she'd started working for her, after being promoted. She thought Allegra had talent and she was grooming her to take on some more experienced authors. Allegra was young, but Pippa thought she had a good eye for books and good instincts about what would sell.

Pippa had a dry sense of humor, which Allegra enjoyed. Allegra asked her if she thought Jane March had a shot at selling the manuscript for a movie. After she read it, Pippa agreed. She called Charlie Zang, a dramatic agent she knew at the William Morris Endeavor Agency, and sent it over to him. Two weeks later, he called Philippa and said he wanted to show it to some producers to option the book, and get it made as a movie. The author was overjoyed, and her literary agent was pleased too. Jane was a young girl from Utah who had written a dazzling book. She was deeply grateful to Allegra for having brought it to Pippa's attention, and Charlie Zang's, with a very exciting, hopeful result. One of the Hollywood producers Charlie knew optioned it. The author got very little money for the option since she was an unknown and the book was as yet unpublished, but if they made it into a film at a later date, she'd be well on her way.

Allegra invited Jane to lunch to celebrate and she asked Pippa to join them, so the two could meet. At Pippa's suggestion, they went to P. J. Clarke's, and the author was thrilled. The two young women had Pimm's cups, and Pippa had a dry martini, which seemed very grown-up to them. It felt like a very sophisticated lunch to Allegra and Jane. She told them she'd been raised Mormon, had eleven brothers and sisters, and had grown up in Salt Lake City, Utah. Coming to New York and getting her book optioned were the most exciting things that had ever happened to her. Allegra was happy for her.

Jane had left Salt Lake when she graduated from Brigham Young University two years before. She was working in a bookstore in Greenwich Village and avoiding her family, who wanted her to come home. She was working on a second book. Her personal story was fascinating to Allegra. Contrary to church rules more than a century old, her grandfather had broken with the church and had become the leader of a small fundamentalist group that engaged in polygamy. He had had four wives simultaneously, and twenty-one children, of which her father was the youngest. Jane March was twenty-four years old.

"You should write about that," Pippa told her over her second martini. "People would be fascinated. Write about what you know," she advised.

"I didn't think anyone would believe me if I wrote about my family. It sounds so weird to normal people. Even Mormons frown on polygamy and outlawed it."

"People are mesmerized by stories about things like polygamous relationships," Pippa assured her, as they ate their hamburgers and drank their way through lunch. They were all slightly drunk by the end of it, but were still making sense. Philippa was convinced that Jane's family would be fertile material for a book.

"My parents keep sending missionaries to show up at the bookstore where I work to talk me into coming back. I'm afraid I'm going to get fired," she confided.

"If Charlie Zang at WME can sell your first book as a movie and if it gets made, you can quit the bookstore job," Pippa reassured her. "And Allegra will find you a publisher for it."

"Even if they don't make a movie of it, I'm not going home," Jane said. She was a pretty girl with dark hair and big brown eyes and girl-next-door looks. She had four roommates in an apartment in the Village, and a boyfriend, and she loved living in New York. So did Allegra. The conversation was lively all through lunch. "My grandfather died years ago," Jane said, "and the kids all grew up, although most of them still live around Salt Lake, but his four wives all still live together in the same house. They're like best friends or sisters. One of them is my grandmother. She was the youngest of his wives. I think he was sixty when she married him, and she was twenty-one. She talks about him like he was some kind of god. It's a very strange phenomenon. Polygamy is against church law and has been for years, but in some remoter areas of Utah, there are small groups of fundamentalists like my grandfather, and it still goes on. They're considered outlaws, and the practice of polygamy is frowned on, but it still happens," Jane told Allegra and Pippa. They were fascinated by what she described.

"I wouldn't want to share my husband, if I had one, with a bunch of other women," Pippa said, and Allegra couldn't imagine it either. But Jane seemed surprisingly normal, despite her unusual story.

"I just lost my grandmother in April," Allegra shared with them. She felt relaxed and enjoyed being with them. She worked hard and hadn't made many friends at the publishing house so far. She was introverted and shy.

"I'm sorry," Pippa said politely. "Were you close to her?" She knew very little about Allegra and was curious to know more. Allegra was very private about her life.

"Not really, although a little more so in the past few years. She and my grandfather were very old-school, and not that engaged with children. I really only got to know them once I was in college here in New York. I used to spend school vacations with them when I was in boarding school in Massachusetts."

"Were your parents dead?" Jane asked cautiously, curious about her too.

"No. My father was in the army, in military intelligence. He passed away this year too. He spent my entire life in war zones all over the world. I saw him for a few hours about once a year. He was killed in Iraq just before he was going to retire." Hers wasn't an ordinary story either, and Pippa was intrigued by both of them. Young authors and her protégées at work were substitute children for Pippa. She enjoyed mentoring them. It seemed easier than real motherhood, which had never appealed to her.

"It sounds like you both have some interesting stories to tell," she commented. "Allegra, have you ever thought of writing?"

"Once in a while. I don't know if I have the talent. I've never tried, but I love to read. It was my fantasy life as a child. The characters in the books were my only friends." She was speaking of a lonely life Pippa could only imagine.

"Ninety percent of writing is discipline and hard work, as much as talent. I have a feeling you'd be good at it," Pippa said gently to encourage her.

"I don't know what I'd have to say," Allegra said shyly.

"I think you'd figure it out," Pippa said confidently. "What about your mother? Where was she?"

"She lives in England. She left when I was six," Allegra said matter-of-factly, as though it were a normal occurrence. And to her, it was by now.

"Your father was in war zones all around the world, and you saw him once a year, and your mother left when you were six, and you grew up in boarding school. What I could do with material like that!" Jane said longingly, and all three women smiled. "I could never get a minute away from my brothers and sisters. Your life sounds like a dream." Philippa could guess otherwise. Allegra had led a lonely life, and probably a painful one.

"It never seemed like much to write about," Allegra said modestly. She hadn't processed it with the thought of writing about it, although the idea of doing so intrigued her.

"Do you have a boyfriend?" Jane asked her. "Mine went to medical school at NYU. I hardly ever see him. He's an intern now."

Allegra hesitated before she answered Jane's question. The Pimm's cups had relaxed her usual reserve. "I'm actually married. My husband is in Iraq. He's in the army, in military intelligence, like my dad. They both went to West Point. He wasn't going to stay in the army, but now he has decided to. He loves his job. Working in military intelligence is addictive."

"That must be tough, having him so far away," Jane said, "and in danger all the time." Allegra nodded. It was true. She worried about Shep constantly, particularly after his last leave, when he went back for another tour of duty in Iraq, despite what it was doing to him, which she could plainly see and he denied.

Joy

"He'll be home in a month, in December," Allegra answered.

"Which reminds me," Pippa chimed in. "I give a big buffet lunch on Thanksgiving every year, for people who have no families to go to. You're both welcome if you'd like to come." She jotted down her address on two paper napkins and handed one to each of them. "You both qualify." She smiled at them. Allegra had no family and Jane's was in Salt Lake.

"This is perfect," Jane said, as she put the napkin in her purse. "My boyfriend just started his internship and he's on duty for Thanksgiving and Christmas, of course."

"My husband will be home for Christmas," Allegra said quietly, and didn't add "if I still have a husband by then." In the shape he'd been in when he left, with his nightmares and shaking hands, there was no telling what condition he'd be in when he got back.

They left each other on the sidewalk outside P. J. Clarke's. Allegra and Jane had both had a wonderful time, and Pippa had enjoyed getting to know them with their confessions over lunch. Allegra's life sounded brutally lonely to her, and Jane's overpopulated, as one of twelve children, although she made it sound like a TV sitcom. But it hadn't been funny all the time, and she had mentioned that her father was a tyrant, and her mother never stood up to him to defend them. But she had also said that she and her siblings got on surprisingly well. She missed them, but she said she was much happier in New York. Some of her older siblings were old enough to be her parents, and she wasn't as close to them. She was closer to her younger ones, but she hadn't seen them in a year. She couldn't afford to go home on the pittance she made at the bookstore. Even so, she said she loved her life in New York.

Pippa had no children and had been divorced for twenty years, and the gathering she organized every year on Thanksgiving was cozy and warm, and included editors she worked with and others she had met over the years, authors of all ages and categories, people from outside publishing, and new people she collected every year. She had a full, busy life, and had a knack for finding interesting, unusual people, who loved meeting each other for a holiday they might otherwise have spent alone.

Her apartment in the East Eighties was full of eclectic objects she had collected on exotic trips. She loved going to India, had traveled in Nepal, the Middle East, and throughout Asia. She'd made several trips to Morocco and loved to comb the bazaars. The items she brought home were as varied and intriguing as the people she gathered. She knew a young chef, who cooked the meal every year. There was Thai food and Moroccan food, and special treats from around the world, and a beautiful golden turkey, carved to perfection, with three different kinds of stuffing. The meal was a feast for the eyes as well as the palate.

Allegra was happy to see Jane March there. They chatted for a few minutes before they each got lured into other groups for conversations about books and publishing. It was a perfect gathering for people who had no place else to be and no one to spend the holiday with. Pippa's relatives were all in England, and she hadn't grown up with Thanksgiving, so she had a less traditional interpretation of it

Joy

and dedicated herself to making it a special event for others every year. The guests were invited for two o'clock, and by nine that evening, many of them were still there. Some came early, others later, but they settled into small conversation groups by the end of the evening, and Pippa kept the good feelings flowing with carefully chosen French wine, which went well with the varied meal.

Allegra was talking to some of the senior editors when Pippa came by to check on her.

"Having fun?" she asked, and Allegra smiled at her.

"It's the best Thanksgiving I've ever had, and the food was fantastic." There were half a dozen homemade pies by then, all provided by the young chef. Pippa had discovered her at a small French restaurant and hired her every year. And it amused Pippa that a French cook and an English editor concocted an international Thanksgiving that everyone enjoyed.

Allegra left with the last of the guests at ten P.M. Jane had left earlier, and Pippa hugged Allegra when she left. Allegra was sorry Shep hadn't been there. He would have loved it. She had found everyone she talked to interesting and intelligent, with fascinating stories to tell. She didn't feel like the odd man out. No one seemed to have a family they were close to. Pippa had met everyone's needs so generously by inviting them. Allegra had loved every minute of it, and went home feeling as though she had met a room full of new friends and people she hoped to see again. She felt lucky that Pippa had invited her.

Shep called her at midnight, and she told him about it. He'd had Thanksgiving with the officers from the intelligence team in the mess hall. They had turkey and stuffing and all the trimmings they were used to for a traditional Thanksgiving meal, despite their surroundings, and being far from home.

"I'm glad you had fun," he said. "I was worried about you." She thought he sounded sad. It could have been a hard day for her, with her father and grandmother having died earlier that year, and no one to spend the holiday with, but Pippa had saved her, and given her the best holiday of all. Like all holidays, it was hard when you had no family to spend it with, but Allegra never really had. She had always been the add-on, the mercy guest at her grandparents' Thanksgiving meals, the duty they felt they were required to perform, and she couldn't remember the last holiday she had spent with her father. He was never home for Thanksgiving, and rarely for Christmas. Shep said he had spoken to his family earlier, and one of his brothers had come home with his wife and children to spend Thanksgiving with his parents.

"I'll be home in a few weeks," he said to Allegra in a tired voice. She thought he sounded more subdued than usual. He didn't tell her there had been a sniper attack and two of his friends had been killed that morning. He never shared news like that with her. He didn't want to frighten her or worry her unduly, and he wasn't allowed to tell her much. Their conversations had to be neutral. He couldn't share his griefs with her.

Allegra and Shep were planning to spend Christmas alone in New York, go to Boston a few days later, and then come back to New York for New Year's to watch the ball drop in Times Square. They had done it before and loved it. She was starting to look forward to his

Joy

coming home. She hadn't dared to before now. Life seemed so fragile and ephemeral when he was in Iraq. She wondered what kind of shape he'd be in when he came home, if his ten-month tour of duty had corroded him further, or if he was becoming hardened to what he saw there. Neither one was a good scenario, and she wondered how soon the nightmares would start, and if his hands still shook. They were the things she'd seen when he was back in New York with her, and she couldn't judge by phone, except from his tone of voice. But she could never guess the horrors he had seen. And he never told her.

She decorated a tree for him before he came home, as she had done before. There would be no call from her father this year. She didn't know if she'd miss it. She was going to wear her grandmother's ruby heart pin on Christmas, and had worn it to Pippa's for Thanksgiving. Pippa had noticed it and commented on how pretty it was. It was an antique and had once belonged to Katharine Hepburn, which made it seem even more magical and special.

Allegra took the train to Washington the night before Shep was due to arrive in Washington. They both knew the drill. She rented a car in Washington to pick him up on the base and drive back to New York. He was going to be stationed in Washington for several months, and she hoped he had changed his mind about not leaving the army. She was going to do everything she could to convince him not to reenlist in June. She wanted him to leave the military before it destroyed him. She hoped it wasn't already too late. Ten months was a long time. Long enough to create a baby, or destroy a man. And there were no babies in their life, and couldn't be for now. She didn't want one yet. She only wanted Shep to survive, body and mind.

Shep didn't rush toward her when he saw her this time, and she didn't run to him and fly into his arms. They saw each other, and a long, slow smile appeared on his face as she walked toward him. He looked weary and battle-worn. When they were standing in front of each other, he reached out and held her. She looked far healthier and more alive than he did. He put an arm around her and they walked to the rented car. He looked and moved like an old man, and she wondered how long it would take to drag him back to the real world and to feeling normal this time. He got in the car and let her drive. He was asleep within minutes, as she talked to him. He had slept on the plane but he was exhausted. Something in his face softened when he saw the tree she had decorated for him, and then his eyes hardened.

"We don't really need that," he said, pointing to the tree. He was still mourning his recently lost buddies who died in the sniper attack on Thanksgiving, and there had been three more since then. The army was hemorrhaging men in Iraq. But he didn't tell her that, or even mention his lost friends. One of them was the same age as Allegra, but war was the great equalizer. It took whom it wanted, young or old, and left the others to try to glue their souls back together once they got home, so as not to frighten their relatives with the truth over the holidays. He was grateful that Allegra had no relatives they had to visit. He didn't have to put a good face on it with her. He just wanted to be left alone to get through the days as

Joy

best he could. And eventually, he'd start to feel like himself again, whoever that person was now.

After the last ten months, he no longer had any idea who he was and what he believed in, what his moral code was, what his ethics would allow him to do, or even what he wanted in the future. He had violated his own honor code so often that it no longer mattered to him when he did. It was no longer a matter of right or wrong, but simply of survival, and whom you had to kill in order to protect yourself and your unit. The acts they committed were equally shocking on both sides, he had seen men tortured and participated in it willingly. He no longer hesitated when something unthinkable had to be done. You did what you had to do, and he could tell her none of it. He couldn't have described it to her or put it into words. He didn't even have the words for it. There were no lines he wouldn't cross anymore. His morality was on hold until the war was over. It had to be that way, or none of them would survive it, and too many of them were being killed anyway, whatever they believed in, and however they had been before. They were no longer the same men they used to be.

He had spent almost two years in Afghanistan and Iraq by then, and he knew he wasn't ready to come back to the real world he had known before. He was only suited now to live in the gray zone of suspended morality. There were no dreams in that world, no plans, no love, and when you went home on leave, you had to fake it until you went back to that gray world again where anything could happen and did every day.

The nightmares started the night he came home. His hands no longer shook, but there was a smoldering look in his eyes, a searing glance. He was burning up from inside. He threw the Christmas tree away the next day. It felt like a symbol of everything he no longer deserved.

"Christmas trees are for kids. We're not kids anymore," he told her, and she quietly put the decorations away. She didn't put the Christmas music on. All he wanted to do was watch TV and sleep. They went for a walk, and he didn't speak to her until they got home. There was no point pretending he was the same. He wasn't. A man with Shep's dog tags had come home, but it wasn't Shep, or anyone she knew.

"You're going back, aren't you?" she asked him when they lay in bed in the dark, on his second night home.

He didn't answer her for a full minute. "I have to," he finally said. "I don't belong here. I thought I could come back, but I can't. At least I'm useful there."

"I need you here, Shep," she said, with tears in her eyes. "I need you to come home, for real. Not like my father, for a few weeks and then leave for a year again. You can't run away." She knew it would destroy him forever if he did, just like it had her father. Shep was a gentler person than her father had ever been. She could tell that Shep was suffering deep within, but she couldn't get to the wounds to soothe them this time. He wouldn't let her. He was rough when he made love to her, and his nightmares were so terrifying that he screamed out in agony in the night. When she tried to wake him up, after he'd been home for a week, he leapt on top of her, crushing her, with a choke hold on her throat as he shook her. She screamed until he tightened his grip and she couldn't make a sound, and then he woke up and looked down at her and jumped away. He cowered in

Joy

a corner, realizing what he'd done, as she fought for breath. He was terrifying. He had become a killing machine in the last ten months, filled with anger and fear. He locked himself in the bathroom afterward and cried, and when he came out, she was sitting on the couch in a bathrobe. The marks of his hands were still on her throat, and she could barely swallow. Their eyes met and there was raw pain in his, and despair in hers. She didn't know how to bring him back this time.

"You need to get help, Shep," she whispered to him. "I know this happens to other people. It's not just you. Will you go to see someone?"

He shook his head. "It won't change anything. It's too late." He sat, his shoulders slumped. He couldn't even look at her again. He was too ashamed of what he had become and what he had almost done to her.

"For God's sake, Shep. Don't go back. Stay and get help."

"It won't change anything. What if I kill you in your sleep one night, like I just almost did?" There were tears in his eyes when he said it. He still loved her, but there was too much venom in him now. He was afraid of himself, and for her.

"You can get help. I'm your wife. I love you. I'm here."

"You shouldn't be. You don't know me anymore." He didn't know himself either, which frightened him. He had brought a monster home to her, like a disease. The monster was inside him and controlled him. He was afraid to go to sleep after that, and only slept in the daytime, when she was awake.

She had taken time off work to be at home with him, but they didn't leave the apartment. He slept by day and prowled the apartment at night, refusing to lie down with her, afraid he'd lose control again during a night terror. He looked exhausted, with dark circles under his eyes. He refused to go to Times Square with her on New Year's Eve, as they'd done before and had planned to. She had bought a small bottle of champagne and he didn't touch it. He bought a bottle of tequila and took a few swigs from time to time. It helped him relax. He hardly ate, and she could see he was losing weight even at home. He'd been back for ten days and looked worse than he had when he arrived, and she could sense that he was eager to leave.

He stayed for another week of sleepless nights and exhausted days, sleeping off the tequila he drank. And then he told her he had to go back to Washington.

"I'll drive you," she volunteered, and he shook his head. She had to go back to work, but was going to call in sick. "You're exhausted." So was she, from watching him constantly, checking for danger signs. He had a temper he'd never had before, and a short fuse. He got furious over nothing and shouted at her, and then apologized.

"I'll take the train. You have to get back to work." She had babysat for him long enough. He'd been home for almost three weeks of hell for both of them. He had come back as a dangerous animal, and they both knew it. A rogue lion, ready to kill her in an instant. She was afraid of him, and tried hard not to be. At times there was a moment, a few seconds of tenderness, when he was the man she had married and the boy she had loved. She knew he was still in there, and she wanted Shep to find him again, and send away the wild beast that he had become. But Shep was both men now, and he couldn't separate them, or control either one. The glimpses of the old Shep were rare.

Joy

"I can get additional time off," she reassured him. "I'll come to Washington with you. You're based there till June. You can get help until then." He looked at her blankly, like she was speaking another language he didn't understand, and didn't want to.

"I need to go back to Baghdad. They need me there."

"I need you here," she said, more sharply than she intended. But she needed him whole and sane, and he was far from it. He shouted in his sleep whenever he slept, and woke up drenched in sweat, the bed soaking as though he had emptied buckets of water onto it. She quietly aired the mattress and changed the sheets when he got up.

"Why do you want me around?" he asked her bleakly in one of his saner moments, with eyes filled with regret.

"Because I love you and I'm your wife," she said without hesitation. She had saved a lifetime of love for him, and it wasn't close to running out. She intended to see this through until he was sane again. She was sure he could be cured. Other wars had created men like him, and many had been healed. She was sure that love could do anything. She was willing to try. She refused to give up on him. Philippa called to see how she was, when she extended her Christmas leave saying she was sick.

"I'm okay," she told her, but she didn't sound it.

"Is it him? Did he come back in bad shape?" Pippa asked, concerned. She knew that Shep was coming home. Allegra had been living for that all year.

"He's all right. It's always an adjustment when he comes home," Allegra said, trying to sound more cheerful than she felt.

"Is there anything I can do to help?"

"No, we're fine," Allegra said, trying not to cry. She didn't want anyone to know how bad he was, and there was no one to tell. There was nothing Philippa could do. He needed to go to the professionals in the army who saw men like him every day, men who were broken from what the army expected them to do. Only they could heal him now. She knew it, and Shep refused to admit it. He didn't want help. All he wanted was to leave, before he hurt her again or did something even worse.

He did try to choke her again one night, when he fell asleep on their bed watching TV, and she lay down next to him, just to feel his warmth beside her for a few hours. The same thing happened during another night terror, and he almost succeeded that time. She was losing consciousness by the time he woke up. He made sure she was all right, and then locked himself in the bathroom for several hours. She was afraid he would do something drastic and begged him to come out. Her voice was hoarse, and when he emerged, he was wearing his uniform. He was clean and shaved, and looked orderly and sane.

"I'm going back to Washington," he said, with the whole story of what had happened in his eyes. "I don't want to hurt you, Allegra. I can't stay here." She didn't argue with him. She knew it was true.

"I'll go with you," she insisted. "You need to be in a hospital, Shep."

"Yeah, a psych hospital," he said with wild eyes, "like a lunatic." He hated himself at that moment, for what he had done to her.

"You're not a lunatic. You have PTSD, battle fatigue, whatever you want to call it."

"So does every soldier in Iraq. You can't put them all in a hospital." The others weren't trying to choke their wives during their night terrors. But they were expected to kill people almost every day. Shep didn't even know who the enemy was anymore. It was him.

"I'll call you from the base," he said coldly. His bag was packed and his mind was made up.

"Why won't you let me come with you?" she asked, pleading with him, her voice hoarse from his attack.

"Because this is up to me to deal with. You don't deserve this," he said quietly, and almost seemed normal for a moment. The Shep she knew was still in there somewhere, being held captive by the sick one. His eyes gazed at her longingly, but he didn't approach her or try to kiss her. She wanted to put her arms around him and comfort him, and she knew she couldn't. He wouldn't allow it. He was too afraid to lose control again, maybe while he was awake this time. Neither of them knew what he was capable of at the moment.

He walked to the door with his duffel bag in his hand. He had packed everything he'd brought with him. He wasn't due back in Washington for another week, but he knew he had to go now. He turned back to look at her, didn't say a word, and left the apartment. After he was gone, she realized he hadn't said goodbye. He didn't know what to say to her, so he said nothing. She heard his footsteps echoing down the stairs as she stood there, and memories of her mother flooded back to her. Shep had forgotten to say goodbye too. Allegra hoped it meant he was coming back, and this was just a bad time they had to get through. She tried to be brave, but she cried anyway. She felt as though she had lost the only man she had ever loved, and who loved her.

She wasn't ready to give up. She was going to fight to save him, and bring back the Shep she knew and loved. She loved the sick one too, but he was dangerous. They both knew it. She was shaking when she sat down on the couch, remembering the look in his eyes when he left, as tears rolled down her cheeks. All she could think of was that she had been braver when she was six. But it had been seventeen years of hard road since then. She could face anything except losing Shep. Everyone she had ever loved had abandoned her, and now Shep too. She prayed she wouldn't lose him, and was terrified she already had. A stranger had returned from Iraq this time, and had taken the Shep she loved with him, and left her all alone again. It was a special kind of hell she knew only too well. And it was Shep's hell now too.

Chapter 8

After a sleepless night, the day after Shep left, Allegra took the train to Washington. She tried to get an appointment with Shep's commanding officer, but he was too busy to see her. She was no one, just a young officer's wife. He had more important things to do, but she was finally able to see a counselor, and told him that Shep was suffering from some form of PTSD and needed treatment. She related the incidents that had occurred when she tried to wake him from his night terrors to comfort him. The counselor listened quietly, and didn't look surprised.

"Some of the men have a hard time adjusting when they come home. There's an element of culture shock, and in some cases battle fatigue. Most of them get over it once their tour of duty is over. If Captain Williams is found to be suffering from PTSD, he will probably spend some time here in Washington before he gets reassigned to a combat zone." He looked unimpressed by what Allegra had said, didn't seem to believe her, and treated her like a naïve young girl. She didn't want to show him the bruises on her throat as proof. She didn't want to get Shep in trouble, or humiliate him, she wanted to get him help. Instead, she told him that her grandfather was General Tom Dixon, and who her father had been. That impressed him more. But in spite of it, he assured her that Shep had had no problem carrying out his duties in Iraq, and had shown no signs of what she described. She got nowhere with him and went back to her hotel.

She tried to call Shep, but he didn't return her calls. He finally called her and was angry about her seeing the counselor.

"What were you trying to do? Get me locked up or put in a psych ward?"

"I was trying to get you help." Her voice cracked as she said it, as she felt desperation filling her lungs. "I don't want you to drown from what they're having you do over there."

"It's too late for that, Allegra," he said sadly.

"What are you going to do now?" But she already knew before he answered.

"I'm going back. I belong there now. I don't want to hurt you. I could have killed you on either of those nights. I didn't even know who you were, until I'd nearly choked you to death." She was fully aware of that. She had known all along that the army would ruin him. He wasn't a born killer like her father, and it had damaged even him. He was unable to feel anything for another human being, not his daughter, his parents, or his wife. Allegra didn't blame her mother for leaving him. She blamed her for not taking her with her when she left. But Isabelle had viewed leaving Bradley as a convenient escape route to get rid of her daughter too. That was what Allegra

Joy

reproached her for, not divorcing her father. She would have divorced him too, or never married him in the first place. Isabelle hadn't understood what she was getting into. Allegra understood it all better than her mother ever had. And she didn't want to lose Shep now. She wasn't running away, she wanted to stand by him.

"I don't want you to go back to Iraq," she begged him. "Can I see you?"

He hesitated, and then sounded harsh when he answered. "No, you can't. Wasn't that enough? What more do you want? For me to kill you in my sleep the next time I have a nightmare? Forget me, Allegra. I'm not the boy you fell in love with at sixteen in Newport. That boy is dead."

"You're the man I married," she said staunchly.

"No, I'm not." He firmly believed that. "I don't know where that man is anymore. He got lost in the last two years. He's not coming back, Allegra."

"He can if you stay here and get help."

"What can they do, make me unsee everything I've seen over there, forget what I've done, what they had me do? I've killed people, I've seen men tortured. I've ordered some to be tortured. You don't forget that." He was crying and so was she. "I have to go back. I belong there now. If I come back to you, I'll end up hurting you sooner or later. You're young, you've got your whole life ahead of you. You'll find a better man."

"I have nothing without you, Shep. I'm begging you, don't give up on us. Don't go back."

"You don't even know who I am anymore. And neither do I." Everything she feared had happened. Her worst nightmare had come true. They had ruined him, broken him. She could feel him slipping through her hands like a drowning man, sliding below the surface. "I have to go," he said in a dead voice.

"Don't go away again, Shep. Will you see me tomorrow?" He didn't answer. "Please," she whispered.

"I'll call you," he said, and a minute later he hung up. She lay awake all that night, waited to hear from him all the next day in her hotel room, and called him that night. The person who answered the phone in his barracks said he was gone. The way he said it sounded odd to Allegra.

"Gone where?"

It wasn't a secret, so he knew he could tell her. "He flew to Baghdad this morning." It sounded like a death knell to Allegra. It also meant that he already knew he was leaving when they'd spoken the night before. He had requested to go back, otherwise they wouldn't have sent him back so soon. She knew how that worked, from her father.

"Thank you," she said in a crushed voice, and hung up. He was gone, without seeing her again. She took the last train back to New York. She couldn't spend another night in the hotel room.

She got back to her apartment at two A.M. She felt dead inside when she walked into her apartment. His civilian clothes were in the closet, but nothing else. She lay down on the bed where he had attacked her. She didn't blame him for it. She knew he was sick. And Shep knew it too. The army denied it. He was much sicker than they realized. They had seen it a thousand times before. It didn't surprise them. If he hurt someone they'd have to deal with it, but until then, as long as he continued to function and did what they needed him to do, they would turn a blind eye. If they sent everyone home who was damaged by the rigors of what they had seen in places like Iraq, where all the rules were different, there would be no one left on the ground to do the job. Shep had gone back to do the job for them, and he had abandoned Allegra. He loved her too much to stay with her. He had told her she deserved better, but she wanted him. She loved him, and she was his wife. He was her family as well as her husband, and the only piece of her history she had left. She had loved him for seven years, since she was sixteen years old. She loved him with all the love she had to give and that no one had ever wanted. And now Shep didn't want it either. He was giving it all back. He didn't want her to love him anymore. It was his final gift to her. And he was leaving her all alone. It felt like a mortal blow.

With enormous effort and ironlike discipline, Allegra went to work the next day. Pippa thought she looked terrible and asked if she was okay. She was deathly pale with dark circles under her eyes. She had worn a scarf around her neck to cover the bruises she still had. There was a devastated look in her eyes.

"Did your husband go back to Washington?" Pippa asked her gently. It didn't occur to her that he'd gone back to Iraq, and Allegra didn't tell her. She was still hoping he'd come back, that he'd change his mind, or they would see something was off, or he'd break down and they'd send him home. Anything was better than his going back to his duties, for another tour, to worsen the damage that was already destroying him. She was waiting for fate to intervene somehow, magically, but it didn't, just as it never sent her mother back, or made her parents love her.

She knew that Shep had loved her. Initially, he had wanted their secret marriage to protect him, but even her love wasn't powerful enough to save him from what he'd had to face in Iraq. It went too far against the grain with him, it tore his soul right out of him, and turned him inside out. The man who went back to Baghdad wasn't the boy she had met in Newport. A dangerous stranger had taken possession of him, a dragon that devoured him, just as she knew it would. Even men like her father didn't survive it unscathed. Men like her father had sold themselves to the devil years before, even before he had met her mother. The devil Shep had encountered in Iraq ate innocent boys like him for lunch.

Allegra went through all the motions of her job for the next two weeks, with no idea what to do next, except keep working. She wrote Shep a letter in Iraq, telling him how much she loved him. She knew it was a futile gesture, like all the letters she had wanted to write to her mother. She did it anyway, and knew the letter would find him, even if he didn't respond. At least she'd said it. She knew he had loved her before, even if he was no longer capable of it. He had left her to protect her, which was the only way he could still love her, to remove himself completely.

* * *

Joy

She managed to work on two manuscripts and complete them, although she could barely keep her mind on the work. Pippa could see how much pain she was in, but Allegra shied away from close contact with anyone. She didn't want to talk. She was fighting to keep her head above water. She had been through pain before, but never as sharp or as devastating as this. It was like having her heart torn out, or a leg ripped off. She was struggling not to bleed to death, and still hoped that Shep would come to his senses, that what was left of him would come back, even though in her mind, she knew it wasn't likely.

Jane March called to invite her to lunch, and Allegra didn't return the call. She just couldn't. She did her work and that was all. She was deep in her shell, and deeply wounded, just as she had been when her mother had left.

Two weeks after Shep left for Iraq, she got a thick envelope from the army legal department, with a bunch of forms in it. She glanced through them, and it was the final death blow to her heart. Shep had filed for divorce before he left. It was a relatively simple procedure for a short-term marriage. Two years was nothing, and they had no children, and no property. It cited irreconcilable differences as the cause for the divorce. He had written in a regulation amount, based on his army pay, as monthly support for two years, the length of the marriage. She wrote on the form that she declined the financial support. She didn't want money from him. Even if she'd been starving, which she wasn't, she wouldn't have accepted it. It saddened her too that his family had never known about their marriage. Shep had been afraid that his family would object when they married, because they were both so young, and then he had left for Afghanistan, and it seemed simpler not to tell them. Now they would never know that they'd had a daughter-in-law for two years. She was sure that Shep would never tell them, since he was divorcing her.

It felt like the ultimate rejection, as it had when her mother had left her. Isabelle had abandoned her daughter, and now her daughter's husband was abandoning his wife. Allegra's father had abandoned her in his own way. She felt as though she had gotten the wrong start in life. It was a pattern she couldn't seem to break. She had no one now. Not even the grandmother who had been hesitant about her for so long, although Allegra would have embraced her early on, if she'd been allowed to. But she had been an inconvenience to her grandparents until she grew up.

There was always some reason for the important people in her life to abandon her or reject her. But Shep was the only one she had loved, and who had loved her in return. Now he was doing it too. It was the worst blow of all.

It took her three weeks to face them, but she filled out the divorce papers and sent them back. Shep wouldn't respond to anything she sent him. He had totally shut her out. He had been gone for five weeks when she filled out the papers with a heavy heart. She didn't want to be divorced. She wanted to be married to him, and had never had a chance to enjoy their life together. He had married her because he was being sent to Afghanistan and thought that their marriage would magically protect him. Now he was divorcing her to protect her, or so he said. It was all for the wrong reasons, but whatever the reason, he was leaving her alone in the world, with no protection. He wasn't willing to fight for the marriage or get help.

Joy

Instead, he went right back to everything that had damaged him so badly in the first place and sought refuge there. He felt it was the only place he belonged now, with others who were as broken as he was.

The men he worked with in military intelligence were all career army, and they were often married to people who came from military families and knew and accepted that way of life, so they understood what the downsides were. Or they married people from the "outside world," outside the military, and their marriages usually didn't last long, with an absentee husband on the other side of the world. Or they did what he had promised to do, one tour of duty and then looked for a job stateside, in or out of the military. He could have done that but hadn't even tried. The war in Iraq had overwhelmed him, chewed him up and devoured him, and now he was trapped by his own choice.

Allegra didn't know what to do. She had enough money to get by for some time, with what her grandmother and her father had left her. She could live on it long enough to find another job. She liked the one she had at the publishing house, and working for Pippa, and the authors whose books she worked on. But it had all made sense while she waited for Shep to come home, and now it didn't. Everything she did reminded her of him, the apartment where he had spent time with her between tours of duty, the city where she was going to live with him. She no longer had any ties to New York, and nothing to anchor her there except the memories of what might have been and the hopes that had died so brutally when he left. She had nowhere to escape to with the cottage in Newport gone. It had sold very quickly, with all the furnishings, much to Isabelle's relief.

Allegra turned twenty-four in the spring, and she felt like a leaf blowing in the wind. She'd thought about it for two months, and then went to see Pippa after her birthday. She had never explained to her everything that had happened, but Pippa knew something terrible had and didn't want to pry until Allegra wanted to tell her, which she didn't. She felt like a giant failure, a reject. She had flunked and been abandoned again. She wanted to run away and hide, but she had nowhere to run to, and no reason to go anywhere, except her own misery. She had looked devastated for three months before she walked into Pippa's office, after a lonely weekend when she had read about various cities she had never been to. She had lived her whole life on the East Coast: New York, Washington, Massachusetts for boarding school, camp in Maine, Newport to visit her grandparents after camp before she went back to school.

There was no important book publishing to speak of on the West Coast, but she didn't care. She needed a fresh start, a place where no one knew her or anything about her and she could start over. She read about San Francisco, but decided it was too small. There were good tech jobs there, but she had no training for them. The film industry in Los Angeles sounded interesting, but she had no background in that either. In the end, she decided to just pick a place and go there, and look for a job later. And if she hated it, she could always come back.

Pippa had dealt with young editors for many years, and she could tell from the look on Allegra's face and the sag of her shoulders that she hadn't come to deliver good news. She had seen girls beaten by New York before. It was a hard city. She'd seen others leave because of a broken heart, relationships that didn't work out, canceled weddings and engagements, and divorces. But there was something so profoundly sad about the look on Allegra's face that Pippa's heart ached just looking at her. She could see that Allegra had had a tough time for the past few months. The shiny, excited look she'd had in the beginning was gone, and all Pippa could see now was sorrow. She wore it like a shawl around her. Her eyes were full of grief and loss, and even her bright red hair looked suddenly dull. Her hair was pulled into a severe bun, and she hadn't worn makeup in months. She was wearing flat shoes, an old black skirt that hung on her, and a gray sweater she had left over from college and should have gotten rid of when she graduated. Philippa poured her a cup of tea, and waited to hear whatever Allegra was going to tell her. Whatever it was, she sensed that Allegra wasn't going to tell her the whole story, just as she hadn't told her she was married for the first few months she worked there. She was a very private person.

"I get the feeling things haven't been going so well lately," Pippa said gently. "Is it the job?" Allegra shook her head and looked apologetic.

"No, the job is fine, and you've been wonderful to me. And I like most of the authors I work with. With a few exceptions." She smiled, Pippa laughed, and knew who they were. She had a few difficult old ones, but someone had to edit them, and Allegra had always been a good sport about it, and never complained. "It's me. Some things have changed in the last few months." She took a breath before she went on, and Pippa waited. She was a patient woman and good with young people. She was used to listening to their problems. "Shep decided to stay in the army and went back to Iraq. He's having . . . he's dealing with some issues around his work in a combat zone. His leave over Christmas didn't go well. He needs help and he doesn't want to get it. He filed for divorce when he left," she said with a heartbreaking glance at her boss.

"Oh, Allegra, I'm so sorry. I know that must be hard," Pippa said. "I wish you'd told me."

"There's just nothing here for me now, except this job. I don't want to stay in the apartment. He's not coming home, not to me anyway. I have nothing to look forward to here. My father's gone, and my grandparents. I have no family. I don't know where to go." Tears filled her eyes as she said it. "I need a change. I'm thinking of going to Los Angeles to see how that feels."

"I thought you loved books and publishing," Pippa said.

"I know, I've thought about it. Maybe movies. Maybe I'll be a waitress," Allegra said, looking lost.

"I think you can do better than that. Starting fresh might be fun, but the geographic solution isn't always the right one. You'll take your problems with you." Pippa was thinking that Allegra needed the right man, or a more challenging job. She was a very bright young woman, and a talented editor. Her biggest problem was that she didn't have a single human being in the world to care about her. It wasn't fair, but it was the hand she'd been dealt, and Pippa could sense that she was trying to make the best of it. It wasn't easy, and never had been. Her mother had given her a push in the wrong direction at a very early age, and her father's defection hadn't helped, or cold, elderly grandparents, none of whom really wanted a child underfoot. And now her deeply troubled and emotionally damaged husband was divorcing her. It was a terrible blow for her. Pippa could see it on her face.

Joy

"Wherever you go, you can always come back," Pippa reminded her. "You're not stuck wherever you are. I assume you have enough money to hang on for a while, so you don't have to take a job you hate."

Allegra nodded assent. "I don't have a lot, but I have enough to live on if I'm careful. I refused Shep's offer of support. If he doesn't want me, I don't want his money, and his parents aren't keen on me. They don't even know we were married. He wanted to keep it a secret until he came home from Iraq and we settled down here and both had decent jobs. But he changed his mind about leaving the army, so we never told them. We wanted to prove to them how responsible we were. And now I'm the only one here," she said sadly.

"Why L.A.?" Pippa asked her. "Do you know anyone there?" She was curious.

"No one. I looked at some employment ads, and they sound okay. There seem to be a lot of agencies to find jobs. The rents look reasonable, and the weather is good." Everything she said made sense, but to take on a new city, knowing no one, at twenty-four, sounded ambitious to Pippa. Allegra was a strong girl and she could see her managing, and doing okay, if she didn't panic. She had a good head on her shoulders. Pippa had seen evidence of it in the seven months she'd worked for her.

"If it doesn't work out, and you come back, I want to make it clear to you that I would hire you back in a hot minute. You're a very capable editor, Allegra. And I suspect you've got some writing talent of your own, if you ever decide to exercise it. I have great faith in you." There was a lot of competition for jobs at her age, but Allegra already had seven months of experience, and Pippa was going to give her a good reference. She was a bright, attractive girl. Someone would hire her.

Pippa just hoped she'd come across a decent person, and go to a good agency. She urged Allegra to be careful of that, and she nodded. Pippa wanted her to find a great job and a new life that made her happy.

"When do you want to leave?" Pippa asked her, hoping it wouldn't be too soon, so she could train another person to take her place. It would take time to find a reliable replacement.

"I have to give up my apartment in ten days if I'm leaving. I was thinking two weeks. I can stay at a hotel for the last few days." Pippa wasn't thrilled at the short notice, but it was respectable. She nodded, genuinely sad to see Allegra go.

"So that's it, I guess. Will you promise to stay in touch? I want to know what you're doing, who you're working for, and what kind of job you get. Don't just forget about us," she said, sounding like a concerned aunt, and Allegra was touched. There wasn't a single other person on the planet who cared about what she was doing or where she was going, not even Shep, after eight years in his life. It felt good that someone did care. Allegra had always kept to herself and had few friends. The only person she was close to was Shep.

"Thank you," she said. Pippa hugged her and Allegra struggled not to cry. She wanted to be brave.

They gave Allegra a little farewell party with a cake in the editorial department, and she was very touched. Pippa had organized it. Allegra had packed up everything in her apartment by then. She had

Joy

sent all her furniture to Goodwill, where most of it had come from, except for the new pieces she had bought for Shep. She got rid of all of it. She wanted no souvenirs of their life together now. She gave away her books at work. She sent everything of Shep's to his parents in Boston, without explanation. He could tell them whatever he wanted to, when they asked him where it came from. Her few kitchen utensils and the toaster and microwave went to Goodwill too.

She had three suitcases of clothes, most of which she used for work and would be too warm for L.A., but she had nowhere to leave them, and she'd need clothes to work in once she found a job. They were all severe-looking skirts and sweaters, some blouses, shoes, a few purses, and a warm coat. She wasn't extravagant and hadn't needed a fancy wardrobe in publishing. She could buy what she needed when she found a job. She found that it was easier and faster to take a life apart than to build one. She had no souvenirs of her father either except his medals, in a box that fit easily in her suitcase, and she had an envelope of photographs of her parents. She didn't have many of those either. Her life was eminently portable. It was a defining statement, how little she had accumulated. She had kept the photographs of her and Shep, and put them in a separate envelope. She wasn't going to look at them. She just liked knowing she had them. She had spent a third of her life with him.

She felt emotional when she said goodbye to Pippa.

"Remember, you can come back whenever you want to. We'll find a place for you," Pippa said, and meant it. "And Allegra, make sure that wherever you land, people treat you right. You deserve it. You feel like you have no roots right now, but you will one day. This won't happen to you again, like it did with Shep. He's a casualty in his own life, which is why you got hurt." She was sad as she watched Allegra get in the elevator, and Allegra was too. For now, Pippa was her only friend, and she was a good person. There hadn't been many in her life.

Allegra got on the plane to Los Angeles the next morning, and watched New York shrink from sight. She was excited and sad at the same time. She hoped Pippa was right, and this wouldn't happen to her again, having no home, and nothing to anchor her. The next time she gave her heart, it had to be someone who would take good care of it, and not walk away and forget to say goodbye, like her mother and Shep. She was worth more than that. For the first time she believed it, even if she'd had no evidence of it yet. She felt like a balloon everyone had let go, and she was rising into the sky, floating on the wind, alone.

Chapter 9

Los Angeles seemed big and confusing at first. Allegra wasn't sure where to go or where to stay, and decided not to look for an apartment until she found a job. She realized from how spread out the city was that she would need a car. She rented one at the airport from one of the places that offered low-priced deals, and headed for the hotel she had found an ad for before she left New York, which rented rooms by the week in Santa Monica, near the beach. She liked the idea of living on the ocean, at least for now. The day after she got there, she sat on the beach, in jeans and bare feet, soaking up the sun. It felt more like a vacation than a search for a new home.

She spent the weekend exploring various parts of Los Angeles, like West Hollywood and Beverly Hills, which would be too expensive to live in. She drove to Malibu on Sunday and saw the enormous beach homes there. Santa Monica had a cozy feeling to it, but might be too far from work. She was surprised by how much driving she did, but she liked it. She had a feeling of freedom, and it was totally different from New York. New York had still been chilly when she left, and the weather was warm and balmy in L.A. She was pleased with her choice so far.

Her mind kept wandering back to Shep as she looked around. She kept seeing things she wanted to tell him about and show him, and she kept having to remind herself that he was gone. He was no longer part of her life and didn't want to be. She had to get used to the idea that she was totally alone in the world again. She knew that she could call Pippa if she ran totally aground, but she wasn't going to let that happen. She was determined to make her new life work and make it a success. She wasn't going to write to Pippa until she found a job and a place to live. For now, she had options, and only had to please herself.

Allegra had been on her own before, but never quite as completely as this. She'd always had a tie to someone, her father in some distant place, and her grandparents, although they weren't affectionate or attentive, but they were there. Her mother had never been an option. For the past eight years, she could reach out to Shep, but now she had no one, not a soul on the planet who cared about her, except Pippa, and she was three thousand miles away and had been her boss, not a friend. It was terrifying and liberating, all at the same time. She had never been this totally free before. She didn't have to please anyone but herself. All the decisions were hers.

Allegra had looked up the employment agencies and had no idea which ones were best. She noticed one that had the most appealing ad. It seemed like a big agency, and offered lots of options. They claimed to handle jobs in tech, startups, entertainment, advertising,

Joy

and various creative fields. There was no mention of publishing, as all the big publishing houses were in New York, but the entertainment industry appealed to her, as did "creative fields," which seemed like a catchall phrase that could mean anything. She decided to call that agency first, and said she was looking for a job. A very professional-sounding receptionist told her to fill out the questionnaire on the website, and then call back for an appointment with one of the agents.

It took Allegra an hour to answer all the questions about her education, job experience, family background, criminal check, and wish list for what kind of job she was looking for, and salary range. She based it on what she'd earned as a junior editor in New York, which didn't sound like a lot.

She went for a walk on the beach after she sent it, and then called the agency back two hours later. She wasn't sure an agent would have seen it yet, but she thought she should check. The same receptionist answered, and asked her to hold for a minute. She called around to see if anyone had processed the application, and one of their senior agents had, and told the receptionist to give her an appointment for ten A.M. the next day. There were several things about Allegra's answers that intrigued the agent, and she wanted to get a look at her, and see if she was for real, and how she presented herself, before she matched her up with any of the jobs they had listed. By sheer luck, Allegra had reached out to one of the best and busiest agencies in L.A. The receptionist came back on the line and gave her the appointment time for the next day. Allegra was pleased by the fast response.

"And who am I meeting with?" Allegra asked.

"Carly Forrest. She's one of the owners," the woman said. The firm was Forrest, Duvall, and Stein. Allegra thanked her and they hung up, and she went back to her hotel room feeling pleased. Things were moving, or at least starting to. She looked through her suitcases to figure out what to wear the next day, and opted for a navy linen suit, with a simple white blouse and high heels, though not too high. There was an iron and ironing board in her room, and she pressed the blouse and suit. She was surprised that she wasn't scared. She was excited to be going to the interview, and wondered what kind of jobs Carly Forrest would send her out for. She wasn't sure where her experience as an editor would apply. She'd have to wait and see.

She had trouble sleeping that night, and watched TV until she fell asleep. She had to keep pulling her mind away from Shep. She couldn't tell him about the interview or ask his advice afterward, as she had when she was job-hunting in New York. This time she was here because of him. If he hadn't destroyed her life in New York, pulled the rug out from under her and filed for divorce, she would never have been in Los Angeles, trying to build a new life, so there was nothing more to say to him. It was hard to get used to, after eight years of looking up to him. Now that all had to change. She was entirely on her own.

Carly Forrest was a tall, slim, blond woman with a good haircut, in a beige pantsuit and high heels. Allegra could feel the agent looking her over thoroughly, and hoped she approved. The navy suit she'd worn looked more like New York than L.A., but it was businesslike and subdued.

Carly asked her a long list of very specific questions that hadn't been on the form, and then sat back and looked at Allegra. She found her intriguing.

"May I ask you, Allegra, what brought you to L.A.?" Carly was interested and paid close attention. "Was it a man?" It was, but in reverse. When Shep abandoned Allegra, she gave up her New York life and came west, but she didn't say it.

"No, it wasn't," she said simply.

"Do you have friends here, or family?"

Allegra shook her head. "No, I don't. I wanted a change, and this seemed like the right place."

"Do you think you'll stay?"

"I hope so. I like what I've seen so far. I've never been here before."

"Were there things you didn't like about your job in New York?"

"No, I loved it. I liked working in publishing, and I know there is no significant publishing industry here."

"We have some magazines, if something comes up from that quarter. You have a lot to offer someone, Allegra, an excellent education at a great private boarding school, a degree from Columbia, and a glowing reference from your first job. We have a number of clients who would be interested in you, if you'd be interested in the jobs. Unfortunately, nothing that would use your editing skills at the moment. We get a lot of calls from celebrities for assistants. Those can be very demanding jobs that would infringe on your personal time. In L.A. a lot of people in the entertainment industry take advantage of their assistants' personal time and call them at all hours. Are you flexible about time?"

"I think so. I don't mind working long hours, unless they call me at four A.M.," Allegra said, joking.

"Some do," Carly Forrest said. "We discourage it, of course, but it does happen, depending on the employer. I have some job descriptions for you to check out." Carly printed out four sheets of paper and handed them to Allegra for her to read. One was as the manager of a trendy restaurant, which Allegra didn't want to do. It required long nighttime hours, and she had no experience for the job. Another was as a personal assistant to a well-known movie star. Carly added the caveat that the actress required flexible hours, she wanted her assistant on call at all hours, and the job required travel. Carly said that the job was very well paid, but very demanding, and there was a clothing allowance that Allegra didn't care about. Her needs weren't extravagant.

There was an older famous Hollywood couple looking for an assistant to share. They were in their eighties and led a very quiet life. Carly was concerned that she might be bored, but the husband was writing his autobiography, so there might be editing involved, which Allegra liked.

And there was a secretarial position for a bank president, which was strictly nine to five, with no additional time involved.

"They all sound interesting except for the restaurant," Allegra said.

"Would you be interested in interviewing for the other three?" Carly asked her.

"I would," Allegra said. She had heard of all three movie stars.

Joy

She had the computer skills the bank president required so she was qualified for the job.

"I'll call them and set it up, and get back to you as soon as I hear," Carly said. She had been very favorably impressed by Allegra, although she was still puzzled by why she had come to Los Angeles with no connection to the city whatsoever. Allegra had said she had no acting ambitions, so she wasn't drawn to it for that. She was a little bit of a mystery to Carly, but she liked everything she saw in the interview. Allegra was polite, well mannered, intelligent, and seemed very professional and mature for her age.

Carly called Allegra at the end of the day. All three clients wanted to meet her. Carly had the acting clients set up for the next day, and the bank president the day after.

"And we'll see what else comes in." She emailed Allegra the addresses, and Allegra left her hotel early the next morning so she'd get to the first interview on time. The actress was the first one, and she lived in Bel Air. Allegra used the GPS to find her house. It was very impressive, and a maid led her upstairs to what turned out to be the star's bedroom. She was in a round bathtub in a pink marble bathroom Allegra could see from the bedroom, and she told Allegra to come in. She walked into the bathroom hesitantly, and the star was naked in the bath. She was a beautiful woman, and very pleasant to Allegra, who was embarrassed to be meeting her naked and tried not to show it, while the star asked her about her previous job and if she was willing to work on weekends. Allegra was trying not to look at her while she answered her questions. Then the star stood up in the round bathtub and asked Allegra to hand her a towel, which she did, trying to look unaffected by it.

"Sorry, I have a meeting with a director this morning and I'm running late. I always do meetings when I'm in the tub. I hate wasting time. Do you have a husband, children, or a boyfriend?" she asked, as she wrapped the towel around her. She had a spectacular body, which Allegra was uncomfortable having seen so much of.

"None of the above," Allegra answered.

"Good. I call at crazy hours sometimes. The agency said you don't mind working late. And you'd travel with me of course. Can you do hair?"

"Hair?" Allegra looked blank.

"You know, hair!" she said, piling her blond mane on her head. "I take a hairdresser with me for press events and red carpet. For personal events, you can do it for me. Your hair is a great color, by the way. I've always wanted to be a redhead."

"Oh, thank you," Allegra said, still startled to discover she'd have to double as a hairdresser on occasion. The job seemed to be more personal than assistant, and Allegra could easily imagine two A.M. calls. The star seemed to expect Allegra to have no life of her own whatsoever. It sounded way more invasive than what she wanted to deal with, particularly the meetings while she was in the bathtub.

She extricated herself from the interview politely while the star wandered around her bedroom naked with her underwear in her hand, but she still hadn't put it on when Allegra left. She heaved a sigh of relief and called Carly from her car. The agent was annoyed that the client had paraded around naked and apologized to Allegra.

"I'm sorry. She does that all the time. She's very proud of her body. She never uses body doubles in her movies."

"She has a great body. I was just startled. But she also wants me

JOY

to do her hair. I don't think I'm the right person for the job. I can barely do my own hair." Allegra laughed, and Carly did too.

"I'm sorry, Allegra. This is Hollywood, and you get a bit of everything here. Her last personal assistant was her yoga teacher and her masseuse. She has very broad ideas of what personal assistants do. I think you'll like the Johnsons a lot, and I promise they'll have their clothes on."

Ed and Betty Johnson were both famous actors. He was well into his eighties and looked frail. He was an Oscar-winning actor and director, and she had been a famous beauty in her day and was in her seventies and still beautiful. He was retired and working on his memoirs, and she still took parts in films from time to time. They were a charming couple, attentive and respectful. It was like visiting someone's grandparents, except that they were both big stars. But they acted like normal people. They wanted her to handle their correspondence, make their social and medical appointments, and help him with his book. She wondered if they really needed a full-time person, it didn't sound like the job would fill her day, although they were lovely and she really liked them. She hated to sound picky to Carly, but the work seemed boring. He had said he spent two hours working on his book every morning, and it looked like it would take him another twenty years to finish it. He had only done thirty pages of it so far. He wanted her to retype whatever he worked on that day. It sounded like she'd be finished by eleven o'clock every morning, and sitting idle, waiting for the phone to ring for the rest of the day.

They loved her and wanted to offer her the job. They said she reminded them of one of their granddaughters. It was an incredibly impressive moment, meeting two such famous people in their home environment, but it didn't sound like much of a job. At least she wouldn't have to do their hair and they weren't naked. In one day, she'd had an amazing introduction to three of Hollywood's biggest stars.

The bank job she interviewed for the next day was exactly as described: proper hours, standard work, and after the first two interviews, it sounded very boring. The bank president was extremely professional, very polite, and not particularly friendly. She didn't think she'd like the job or working for him. So, with three strikes, she was out by Wednesday afternoon, and she was discouraged, when Carly called her back after she turned down the bank job.

"I didn't think it was for you, but it shows you a range of what's available right now," Carly said. They were very different jobs and employers. None of them were right for her. Carly could sense that Allegra was discreet and somewhat shy. But there was also a certain gutsiness to her, if she'd come to L.A. knowing not a soul. She was an interesting combination of strong and vulnerable, and Carly wanted to help her find a good job. She was a bright girl, and Carly sensed that she'd be a star herself in the right job. She sounded cautiously excited when she called Allegra back.

"I just got a call from one of my favorite and most difficult clients. He's what I call a recidivist. He's a wonderful employer, a huge talent, and a kind man, but he works incredibly long hours and very hard, and he expects his assistants to work as hard as he does, which isn't possible. He has a bit of a temper but he always apologizes, and he's a gentleman. He expects his assistant to do both business and personal aspects of the job, which means calling his tailor in London and getting his hair cut at home between meetings and setting up

Joy

meetings with his attorney and *The New York Times*. He's a very successful music composer for films. He's won several Oscars. He's sixty-two years old and runs around like he's thirty. He's tireless. His assistants usually quit in six months. He wears them out, and they never last more than a year, so it won't be a long-term job," although Allegra was young enough that she thought she might last, a little longer at least. "He's a human tornado, and he's probably a genius. You'll either love him or hate him, and he knows how demanding he is, and pays his employees extremely well. His name is Henry Platt." Allegra had heard of him, and was intrigued. He had done the soundtracks of some of the most famous movies in Hollywood. "He can see you at six forty-five tonight. He has to be in his studio at seven-thirty, so he won't keep you long. Are you free then?" She was, and it sounded daunting but fascinating.

"Is there anything else I should know?" Allegra asked her.

"He's extremely punctual, and I have a crazy feeling this might work. For a while anyway. See what you think after you meet him. You can call me on my cellphone to let me know. I'll be on my way home, stuck in traffic." Carly gave Allegra the address and wished her luck.

Allegra left her hotel an hour early to be there on time and arrived five minutes early. Henry Platt had a large, imposing house in Bel Air, with a shiny black door and a large brass knocker. A woman in a black uniform with a white apron opened the door and let Allegra in. The house was very formal and reminded her a little of a smaller version of the cottage in Newport, but the atmosphere was friendlier. She could see a large living room, a book-lined library, and a beautifully tended garden outside. Allegra gave her name and was led into the library, where a tall man with a mane of gray hair was putting books away. He was wearing an impeccable light blue shirt and gray slacks, and he had headphones around his neck. There was a grand piano in the room, and stacks of sheet music piled on top of it. He was handsome, with a weathered, lined face, and looked his age, and he smiled warmly when he saw her.

"Ah, you must be the young woman come to save me. Your predecessor left yesterday. She's getting married and moving to Australia. You're not engaged, are you?"

"No, sir."

"I received eighty emails today, and I don't have time to answer them." He sounded like he expected her to take her jacket off and get to work immediately. He seemed like a busy man who would juggle ten projects at once and expect her to do twice as many. "Carly tells me you just moved here from New York. Do you know your way around L.A.?"

"Not yet. I got lost twice on my way here." She smiled shyly.

"You'll learn. I moved here from New York too, thirty years ago. It grows on you. I like the weather." He was friendly, and he had lively eyes that were observing her intently. He looked like a nice man, although she'd been warned about his temper.

"I like the weather too." She smiled at him again. He invited her to sit down, and he asked her all the expected questions about her previous job.

"Why did you want to be an editor?"

"I love books," she said simply.

"Maybe you'll write one."

"I don't think I have the talent. Editing is easier."

Joy

"You never know what you can do until you try," he said, challenging her. "I used to think I couldn't compose, and now that's all I do. I trained to be a concert pianist. What I do now is much more fun. Come, I'll show you." He led her through a door to a fully equipped, space-age sound studio. It was amazingly impressive. "I spend most of my time here. I work a twenty-hour day. Your day will be shorter than mine, but I often keep my assistants past their normal hours. Do you mind staying late if I'm busy?"

"No, I don't mind," she said, somewhat intimidated by him. He was such a big persona. He was a big man with a larger-than-life personality. She was impressed by who he was, but he seemed straightforward and open and wasn't trying to frighten her.

"I do most of my work here at the house. Occasionally, I work in the sound studios of the film studios I work for. You would come with me."

"It sounds very interesting."

"Sometimes it is, and a lot of work," he said, and led her back to the library. "Carly says you have excellent references. I believe her. I need someone right away. There are all those emails to answer. How soon can you start?"

"I'm free now. I just got here five days ago."

"Where are you living?"

"At a hotel in Santa Monica, until I find an apartment." And first, a job, she didn't say.

"That's too far away, you'll be stuck in traffic for an hour getting here. You should try West Hollywood or Beverly Hills."

"I wanted to wait to get an apartment until I found a job," she admitted, when pressed.

"That's sensible. Can you start tomorrow morning? Eight-thirty?"

"Yes, I can," she said. She liked him, and wanted the job. He didn't give her time to think about it, but it felt like the right one, even though she could see that he might be a handful at times, he seemed like the kind of person who wanted everything done yesterday.

"That's settled then. I have a recording session next week. You can sit in on part of it to see what I do. And I have a meeting with a screenwriter tomorrow. We have a busy day, and you have those eighty emails waiting for you. They multiply exponentially at night, so there will be more tomorrow. I hope you're fast, Allegra. You'll have to be to keep up."

"Yes, sir." He didn't try to hide that it would be a lot of work, which she didn't mind.

"That's a little formal, you can call me Henry," although that seemed too informal to her. He was a man of great stature both physically and professionally, and she was somewhat daunted by him, as he walked her to the door. There were delicious smells coming from the kitchen. "Louise is a wonderful cook, she'll feed you on the nights you work late." He reminded her of a good version of her father, the way she would have liked him to be, a benevolent dictator. There was a four-star-general quality to Henry Platt, like her grandfather. She felt as though she had been swept up by a tidal wave, but there was a warm atmosphere in his home, and she felt at ease there. All she had to do was get used to him, and the pace he expected of her. She had a feeling there wouldn't be much downtime in the job, but it sounded fun and exciting and busy. It was just what she wanted, and Carly had told her the salary. It was going to be very easy to live on. He paid as well as Carly said he did. But Allegra could tell that she would have to work hard to earn it. It seemed like a fair exchange. Hard work for good money. She wasn't afraid of working hard, and when he closed the door behind her, she smiled all the way to her car parked outside. She had a job! Her new life in L.A. was off and running. Her only regret was that she couldn't tell Shep about it.

She called Carly from her car on the way back to Santa Monica. She'd have to find an apartment on the weekend.

"He loved you," Carly said, as soon as she answered her phone. "I don't know what you said to him, but he thought you were terrific. He wants you to start tomorrow morning." Carly sounded victorious. She got a big fee from it, but she also liked putting the right people together. It was like matchmaking.

"I know, he told me."

"Don't let him overwhelm you. He moves fast, just follow your instincts with him. He works on a million things at once, and his directions can be confusing. If you don't understand something, ask him. He's actually very human and reasonable. I'm very happy this worked out, Allegra. I think this will be a very good match. You're bright and on the ball, and you'll catch on fast. The first week may be challenging, but you'll settle in quickly."

"I'm not afraid of hard work," Allegra said bravely.

"Neither is he. He'll want you to sign a confidentiality agreement tomorrow, it's just a formality. He's a very private person."

"So am I." It felt like a good match to her too. She hoped he'd be satisfied with her work.

"Good luck," Carly said. "I'm glad we found you something so quickly. And good luck in L.A. Call me if you have any problems, and

I'll whip him into shape," she said, and they both laughed, Allegra because she thought she could handle him, and Carly because she knew Henry Platt would keep her running. But if Allegra was willing to, Carly thought they'd be perfect for each other. She drove home the rest of the way, smiling, and so did Allegra. She had a job in Los Angeles! Her new life was taking off!

Chapter 10

Allegra set her alarm for five-thirty the next morning, to be sure she wouldn't be late, and she wanted to be mentally prepared for her new adventure. She was determined to be fully alert and ready to learn everything she had to. She wore a simple black pantsuit with a white blouse that she had worn for work in New York, with her red hair pulled back in a neat bun. She looked serious and professional. She gave herself a full hour to drive to Bel Air, after his comment the night before about the morning traffic from Santa Monica. She discovered he was right. She arrived at Henry Platt's home exactly two minutes before she was due to start at eight-thirty. She had just made it, she wanted to be prompt on her first day. Particularly since Carly had said punctuality was important to him. He was a stickler for precision, and reliability.

She realized that her hand was shaking when she rang the bell. The same woman answered the door as the night before, in an immaculate white uniform this time, and there was a man vacuuming behind her. The house was already in full activity at eight-thirty in the morning.

"Hello, I'm Louise." The woman smiled at her. She looked like she was somewhere in her fifties, and she seemed warm and welcoming. It was a nice start to Allegra's day and very different from the serious corporate atmosphere at the publishing house in New York she just came from.

"Mr. Platt says you're a wonderful cook," Allegra whispered to her, and Louise smiled again.

"He's easy to please, as long as you serve his favorites," Louise said modestly, and pointed to the library. Allegra thanked her and hurried to the room where she had met Henry Platt the day before. He was sitting at his desk, wearing his headphones, playing silently on an electric keyboard on his desk and stopping to make notes. Allegra didn't want to interrupt him, and stood awkwardly waiting for him to notice her, not knowing what to do. She didn't want to wave at him or make noise. He was deeply engrossed in what he was doing. After a few minutes, he glanced up after he jotted down a note, and saw her. He looked surprised at first, and then he smiled and took his headphones off.

"Sorry. I was preparing something for my meeting later with a screenwriter, for a movie we're working on together. If you go through the studio, you'll find a little office. That's for you, you can leave your things in there. Then come back here and I'll get you started on the emails." He pointed to the door they'd gone through the night before when he showed her the sound studio, and she found the office easily. There was a closet, and she hung up her jacket and left her purse in it. There was a pad and pen on the desk,

Joy

and she grabbed them and hurried back to the library, where he was waiting for her. He was wearing a black T-shirt and jeans and looked informal. But his eyes were bright and alive. He pointed to a chair across from his desk and began rattling off responses to various emails. She managed to keep up with him, but barely.

"Am I going too fast?" he asked her at one point, and she was surprised by the variety of matters he dealt with. A concert in Tokyo he declined, one in the Netherlands he accepted. A speech he agreed to give in Paris, meetings in London in the fall about a movie. The list was long. "Just leave anything personal. It's a short list and I'll deal with them tonight. If you have questions, make a list and I can answer them at lunchtime. I don't usually eat lunch, and if I do, I eat at my desk, unless I have someone here. You can take your lunch hour when you get a break in the action," he said, and she nodded. "Was I right about the traffic, by the way?" he asked her.

"Completely. I'm going to look for an apartment this weekend, as close to here as I can afford," she said. But with the salary he was paying her, her range had broadened considerably. He was paying her almost twice what she had made in New York, and L.A. was a less expensive city. Rents were noticeably lower, she had observed in the ads she'd read in the real estate section of the paper, although she wasn't familiar with all the good neighborhoods and those to avoid. She would figure it out when she saw them. He looked at her for a minute then, before she went back to her office to get started.

"What does your family think about your moving out here? I assume they're all in the East, given your history until now," which was all East Coast. He had read her résumé carefully that morning before she came to work, to get a better sense of her. She had a good education, he had noticed that immediately, just as Carly at the employment agency had. She'd been supplying his assistants for twenty years and knew what was important to him. He liked well-educated, smart young women who presented well, and were ladylike. He didn't want hippies, tattoos, or women who drank heavily or drugged, stayed out till four A.M., and came to work hungover and too wrecked to work. He was a serious artist with a huge career and wanted a capable assistant to help him. He liked what he read on Allegra's CV, and her glowing reference from Pippa. And he liked the conservative way she looked. He could take her to meetings with him.

Allegra hesitated before she answered his question. She didn't want to sound pathetic, but the truth was unfortunately very simple.

"I don't have a family, sir," she said quietly.

"None at all?" He looked surprised when she shook her head. She was young to have lost everyone.

"My father died last year. He was in the military and was killed in Iraq. My grandparents are deceased. I have no siblings, and my mother lives in London." It was a clean sweep except for her mother, and he was relieved for her. She was very young to have no relatives at all. It made her coming to L.A. on her own even more remarkable. There was something about her that suggested to him that she was an unusual girl. Her reference letter from Pippa indicated that to him too, without coming right out and saying it.

"Do you visit your mother often?" he asked, feeling slightly intrusive, but he was curious.

"No, I don't," Allegra said, looking him directly in the eyes.

"Will she come to visit you here?"

Joy

"No," Allegra said simply. The way she said it discouraged him from asking more about her. Allegra made it very clear that she had no family whatsoever. "You won't have to worry about family reunions and events, or holidays. I'm on my own." He wondered if she had come to L.A. for a man. He couldn't think of any other reason why a woman her age would come to a city where she knew no one. But he felt awkward asking her the question.

"Well, I'm very pleased to have you here to help me. I hope you'll enjoy the job and stay until we grow old together." She laughed at the way he said it. "I am old, of course, but I'm planning to work for another forty years, which will make me a hundred and two when I retire, so get ready." She was smiling and so was he.

"I'm all set. And I'd better get to your emails."

"Excellent." He put his headphones on and got back to work, and she left for her office, with the computer set up for her on the desk. He was thinking about her. She was an odd girl, but he liked how straightforward she was, and how brave she seemed, without being aggressive about it. She seemed like a gentle person, but he could tell that she had backbone, and he liked that about her. He wondered what her boyfriend was like, and hoped he was a good guy, and wouldn't cause any problems. That was often how he lost his assistants. They broke up with their boyfriends and left L.A., or they got married like the last one. He also recognized that he worked them hard, because he worked hard himself and kept long hours. He had lost a number of assistants who preferred the more relaxed youth-friendly atmosphere of the dot-com firms in San Francisco, where they could play games with young people their age at lunchtime, show up in shorts and flip-flops, and bring their dogs to work.

He ran a tight ship, and from the serious atmosphere in his home, Allegra felt that she could meet his expectations.

He continued to work at his keyboard and make notes until lunchtime. When he stopped, Allegra reappeared to report to him.

"All done with the emails. There were a hundred and nine. I answered them as you told me to. Seven of them were personal. I sent them back to you so you can respond yourself."

"Are you sure you got all the others done? That's very fast." He looked surprised and a little dubious.

"Yes. I added a brief personal greeting, hoping they're well, and then I told them what you asked me to say."

"Very impressive. Are you always that fast?"

"I try to be." She smiled at him. The personal emails were from people who seemed to be friends, although not close ones. They all mentioned that they hadn't seen him in several months and assumed that he was working on films. So they were more acquaintances than friends. Allegra knew from Carly at the agency that Henry was divorced, and she had noticed a photograph in a silver frame in the library, of two young children, a boy and a girl. The photograph was old and slightly yellowed, and she assumed they were his children. There were no other photographs of them in the room, although there were photographs of him with various celebrities and movie stars. And he had two Oscars on display.

Louise brought him a tray with a sandwich on it, and he told Allegra that she was welcome to make herself a sandwich in the kitchen, or Louise would.

"You can go out if you prefer, but there's no place in Bel Air to eat really, except the Bel Air Hotel, which is rather grand. You'll have to

Joy

go to Beverly Hills if you want to go to a restaurant," he explained. She had noticed that on the way to work. There was no commercial area in Bel Air that she had seen.

"I'll grab an apple and a yogurt in the kitchen, if that's all right," she said simply, and he nodded. He couldn't help noticing that she had a lovely figure and was very slim, so she obviously didn't eat a lot, or maybe she couldn't afford to. He couldn't guess what kind of background she came from, although she was very well brought up and had gone to good schools. But a father in the military didn't suggest money, and her lack of family was intriguing. She didn't seem like a black sheep or a rebel, and she had a very gentle demeanor.

He finished his lunch quickly, as he always did, and was back at work an hour later when she came to report in after lunch. He was in the studio by then, turning on some speakers, and he lit up a large video screen.

"I'm meeting with a screenwriter. We've done several movies together. We're working on two at the moment. He's very talented, Jordan Allen."

Henry asked her to make several calls for him then, for reservations at various restaurants where he was going to have lunch meetings, and one at the Polo Lounge at the Beverly Hills Hotel. She had just finished the calls when the doorbell rang, and a tall, well-built, very handsome young man in a T-shirt and black jeans and motorcycle boots walked into the studio and greeted Henry warmly. He had a kind of cocky, arrogant air, his dark hair was tousled, and he looked to be about thirty-five. He hadn't shaved in a week. It was a look he cultivated, and not a beard he was growing. He glanced over at Allegra and stared at her for a minute. Henry introduced him as the screenwriter Jordan Allen, and she went to the kitchen to order coffee for them both, at Henry's request.

As soon as Allegra left the room, Jordan turned to Henry. "Wow! Where did you find her? You've seriously upgraded your office. She's gorgeous."

"Behave yourself." Henry laughed at him. "She's my new assistant. She just started today, and if you steal her or scare her off, I'll kill you. I've lost two assistants in four months, and I'm desperate."

"Me too. I want her. I need her more than you do. I haven't dated a decent woman in six months, and you're a workaholic. You don't deserve an assistant who looks like that."

"I hadn't noticed," Henry said primly, and Jordan laughed at him.

"I don't believe you. You're not dead, that old, or blind. She's the best-looking woman I've seen in a year, and I work in the film industry. She's wasted on you if you hadn't noticed. How old is she?"

"I forget. Twenty-three, twenty-four, something like that. She just moved here from New York, and I swear if you run off with her, I'll steal *your* assistant."

"You're welcome to her. It's a deal," Jordan said, just as Allegra came back into the room, holding a tray with two mugs of coffee. She set it down where they could reach it, went back to her office, and closed the door. There was a window where she could see into the studio and they could see her. Some responses to her earlier emails had come in, and she went through them, oblivious to the two men in the sound studio. They were both wearing headphones, watching clips of the films they were working on, and Henry played the pieces he was composing for them. They frowned at times, listened again, made notes, Henry would try a different version, or sometimes Jordan loved what he played the first time. It was minute, intense work, and they were in the studio for more than two hours. Jordan had glanced over at Allegra a number of times, and she didn't notice. She was busy with her own work.

After the meeting, Henry walked Jordan out. They both seemed pleased with the result of their time together, and just before he left, Jordan turned to Henry at the front door.

"And don't forget, we're trading assistants. I'll send mine over in the morning. Have yours ready for the exchange." Henry laughed at him. Jordan was a joker and he liked to tease. Women constantly fell at his feet and he took full advantage of it. He was a famous womanizer around town. Allegra had paid no attention to him at all, which amused Henry. She was serious about her work, which pleased him. If she'd flirted with Jordan, he would have been annoyed. He took another look at her then, when he went back to her office after Jordan was gone. He had noticed that she was fresh and young and attractive, but she dressed soberly in a businesslike, non-seductive way, and he had paid no attention to how beautiful she was. Jordan was right. She was striking. But all that did to Henry was make him want to protect her in a fatherly way, not seduce her.

He gave her a mountain of things to type, file, organize, and research as a result of the meeting, and he was surprised when she showed up in the library at six o'clock to tell him she had finished what he gave her. She was ready to leave for the day. Her normal leaving time was five-thirty.

"Already? You can't have done all that by now," he said incredulously.

"I did, sir," she said calmly.

"Carefully? You didn't just rush through it?" He was dubious that she could have done it all.

"I promise. I paid close attention to your directions, and I finished it all."

"You're clearly a magician." He smiled at her. She'd done a good job all day, and she was pleasant and easygoing to work with. There was no drama, she just kept working at a steady pace until all the assignments were complete. She didn't waste time. "You did good work, Allegra," he said seriously. "If you keep this up, we're going to work very well together. Thank you."

"I really enjoyed it. I had a good time today." She liked being able to complete her tasks and move on to the next ones. He kept up a steady flow of projects for her. There was no downtime, no time to think about her own life. It was exactly what she wanted.

"See you tomorrow," he said, and she left. It took her over an hour to drive home to Santa Monica, to the hotel. The traffic was heavier and there had been an accident, which slowed everyone down. Looking back at the day, she loved her new job and she liked her employer. She was delighted with her move to Los Angeles. There were still hard moments at night, when she thought about Shep, and missed him. She worried about him, but he wasn't hers to worry about anymore, and the job was going to keep her busy. Moving away had been the right decision, and things had fallen into place very quickly. She couldn't imagine a time yet when Shep wouldn't come to mind at every opportunity. But at least for now, in the daytime, she wouldn't have downtime to think about him. It was a blessing she was grateful for. She would never forget him, but she

Joy

had to find a way to not think about him anymore. That was a much harder job than any assignment Henry Platt could give her.

Her second day at work was even busier than the first. Henry was in and out of the sound studio all day, and every time he emerged, he had another stack of projects to give her. She didn't stop all day, not even for lunch. She went out to the kitchen for a cup of tea at four o'clock and chatted with Louise for a few minutes, who handed her a plate of cookies to go with the tea.

"You work as hard as he does," Louise commented approvingly. "He doesn't like lazy people." Allegra laughed at the comment. "His last assistant was always putting on lipstick and talking to her boyfriend. She's lucky she quit to get married. He was going to fire her," Louise said matter-of-factly, and Allegra smiled as she helped herself to another cookie.

"Does he spend much time with his children?" Allegra asked innocently, and Louise frowned and lowered her voice to answer her.

"He doesn't see them at all. I've been here eighteen years and I've never met them. They had a very bad mother. They're old now, older than you. I think the mother said bad things about him and they believed her. Now he doesn't want to see them."

"That's sad," Allegra said quietly. She wondered if he missed them, as she thought of the yellowed photograph in the silver frame in the library. They were very young then.

"He never married again. I never see women, except for big parties like the Oscars. He works all the time. He's a good man," Louise said, clearly devoted to him. "He's a good boss, a good person." It spoke well of him that his employee thought so highly of him and admired him so much, Allegra thought.

She wondered what had happened with his children. Louise seemed to have the general gist of it, with a bad divorce, but something really awful must have happened, if he hadn't seen them in the eighteen years that Louise had worked for him. And he seemed like a warm person, not like her own mother. Henry must have been badly wounded by his ex-wife if it had caused a permanent rift with his children. It made her think again of Shep. She was sure he wouldn't have done what he did if they'd had children. But he was so deeply disturbed now that he might have done it even then. He was no longer in any condition to make sound decisions or maintain close relationships. In a way, Allegra was sorry they hadn't had a baby. But she had felt too young, their life was so unstable with him in the army, and her life would have been infinitely harder now if she had a baby to worry about, and a father who had abandoned them. She had lived it. She didn't want that for a child. It was better that they had had none.

"Miss Allegra, are you okay?" Louise stirred her from her reverie. She had gotten lost in thinking about Shep again, and was a million miles away for a minute, and Louise had seen it.

"Sorry, I'm fine. Just thinking about work."

"You looked very sad for a minute. Like someone died."

"No, I'm fine. I just have a lot to do. Thank you for the tea and cookies."

"You need to eat more!" Louise said, in a scolding voice, wagging a finger at her, and Allegra smiled and hurried back to her office,

Joy

pushing Shep to the back of her mind again. The piece of information Louise had shared with her about Henry not seeing his children had been interesting, and a glimpse into the private side of him. He had had her sign the confidentiality agreement the day before. As Carly had said, it was a short standard agreement, which made perfect sense for a man of his position, with her working in his home, and privy to private information, like what she had just learned about him. The agreement was to prevent greedy, ill-intentioned people from selling him out to the tabloids, which could easily happen. She wasn't offended by being asked to sign it.

Despite skipping lunch, she didn't finish her day's assignments until after seven o'clock. Henry was still in the studio when she went to say good night to him.

"I'm sorry it got so late. I finished everything," she said, when he took the headset off. He'd been in the studio all day, and she'd been buried in her office. There had been a never-ending flood of paperwork across her desk.

"Are you in a hurry to get home?" he asked her, and she could see another wave coming toward her. He obviously wanted to give her more. She was tired, but didn't say so, and she hadn't eaten a real meal all day, since she never ate breakfast, just a cup of coffee before she left for work.

"No, it's fine. Is there something you'd like me to do?" She thought he looked tired too. He'd been wrestling with the latest score all day, after his meeting with Jordan Allen the day before.

"Do you like meat loaf?" It was such an odd question that she laughed.

"Yes. Why?"

"Louise makes the best meat loaf in the world. It's my favorite dinner. And I never saw you stop for lunch today. I need a break, and she made meat loaf tonight. Do you want to stay and have dinner? I'm going back to the studio after that." She hesitated. She didn't want to get off on the wrong foot with him by refusing. And he had asked her so kindly. She was tired and wanted to go home, and not prolong the day. It was late, and she'd been there for eleven hours working nonstop.

She thanked him and accepted the invitation. And Louise set two places for them in the dining room. It was a civilized moment that reminded her of Newport again. There was meat loaf, mashed potatoes, and green beans. It was a healthy dinner. She hadn't had anything like it in weeks. She was living on salads and food she bought in a deli near her hotel, or skipping meals entirely. It was a relaxing break for both of them after a long day.

He questioned her about her family. He asked her about her father and his being in the army.

"Did you travel all over the world with him?" he asked, intrigued.

"No, he was in military intelligence, usually in war zones. Iran, Afghanistan, Somalia, the Sudan, Panama, Libya, Bosnia. None of them were places he could have taken me to. He went wherever there was trouble and stayed for a year or two." Henry was surprised.

"So you were with your mother?" he asked her, and she shook her head, enjoying the delicious home-cooked meal Louise had prepared.

"No, I stayed with my paternal grandparents when I was very young, and then boarding school for seven years after they died." It sounded like a lonely life to him, but she looked at ease with herself, and didn't say anything derogatory about her parents, which was unusual.

"Were you happy in boarding school?" he asked, curious about her. She shook her head in answer.

"Actually, I hated it. It was like prison, and I was always the odd man out, the girl who had no family," she said matter-of-factly. "In summer, I went to camp in Maine. And on school holidays, I stayed with my maternal grandparents in Newport, Rhode Island. They had a house there, and the rest of the time they lived in New York. The house was very comfortable, but they weren't thrilled to have a child on their hands. They were quite old by then, but they had a busy social life they enjoyed. I always felt like an intruder." She was so open and honest that it startled him.

"And where was your mother in all this, if you don't mind my asking?" He was trying to fit the puzzle pieces of her life together, and she felt surprisingly comfortable talking to him, maybe because he was so much older, and seemed so benevolent. "Somehow it sounds like your mother wasn't part of the story, with all those grandparents involved, boarding school and camp and an absentee father."

"She wasn't part of the story. She left when I was six. She went to New York and moved to England a year later. So my father had to figure out who to leave me with for a year or two at a time while he was away. He visited me at school between tours of duty before he took off again." Henry was shocked by what she said, and stared at her.

"She just left? Like that? Goodbye?"

"No goodbye." Allegra smiled at him. She looked wise and mature when she did. "She forgot to say goodbye."

"And you never went to visit her?"

"I wasn't invited. I've seen her four or five times in the past eighteen years. She's not keen on motherhood. She was young when she married my father. She was a year younger than I am now when she had me," although not for an instant could Allegra imagine abandoning a child at her age, or any other age.

"You really are an extraordinary person," he said. "That's quite a history. And who is there now?" he asked her gently, almost afraid to ask. But he was as direct and straightforward as she was.

"No one. There's me. My father's parents died when I was eleven, which is why I had to go to boarding school. The others died in the last two years, and so did my father. Which leaves me. My mother is in England, but we really have no reason to see each other. She gave up custody when she left my father. I saw her seven or eight months ago for lunch. We're strangers to each other. I think we both prefer it that way now." She didn't look devastated as she said it. She was used to her history by now, and she had survived it. The one person she left out of the story was Shep. But that still hurt too much to talk about, and he wasn't her family anymore. There was no reason to tell Henry about him, or that she was in the process of a divorce.

"I don't know how you came through all that and are as sane as you are. And you seem very sane to me."

"I hope so," she said quietly.

"Family relationships can be complicated. And some parents do terrible things to their children. I have two children. I went through a very bad divorce thirty years ago. My wife left me for someone else, a film producer I worked with. Our children were very young, and she poisoned them against me. She remarried, moved to Italy,

Joy

and made it impossible to see the kids. By the time that marriage broke up, and I could get near them again, the children believed her. They thought I abandoned them. They didn't believe that she had kept them from me. I don't see them, and they've never wanted to be close to me again. It hurt terribly for a long time, but I've made my peace with it. They don't want me in their lives, and don't need me, and after all this time, I'm all right with it. I'm here, if they ever want to see me again. My ex-wife never admitted to them what she did to prevent me from seeing them for fifteen years. People do terrible things sometimes. It sounds like you were doubly unlucky with your parents. Do you hate them for abandoning you?" he asked her, looking at her intently.

"No," she said quietly. "I don't feel anything for my mother. And I think my father was destroyed from the inside out, from what he did in all those war zones. He was like a killing machine with no heart. That way of life destroys people." She thought of Shep when she said it and felt the familiar tug at her heart. He was the only regret she had, the only wound that hadn't healed yet, but she knew it would one day. If she had healed from losing all the others, she would heal from losing him too. She was determined to now. Her own survival depended on it.

"You're a very strong woman, Allegra. I know what that feels like, losing people you love, a parent or a child. It's like having your arms and legs torn off and your insides ripped out. And then one day you wake up, and you realize that you survived it. The sun shines again, you're still breathing and alive. You work and live and meet people and laugh. My work got me through it. Writing music helps me. Have you ever written about how you felt when you were alone?"

She shook her head. "You should one day. It will free you. But you seem to be doing fine." He had enormous respect for her. They had finished dinner by then, and Louise had left them alone. She could tell that they were talking seriously. "I think I'm very lucky that you showed up for the job. And now you have an employer and a friend in L.A.," he said, smiling at her. She felt sorry for him about his children, but he seemed to have recovered from it. It was a long time ago. She had recovered from her losses, except for Shep, but in time, she would recover from him too. She had to. There was no other choice. Henry Platt seemed like a good friend to have.

Louise topped off the meal with homemade apple pie and vanilla ice cream. Allegra smiled at Henry when they were finished.

"Thank you for a wonderful evening, and a delicious dinner . . . and a job."

"Thank *you* for being brave enough to come to L.A." He smiled back at her.

"You're brave when there's no other choice," she said wisely.

She left a little while later. It had been an amazing evening, with their exchange of confidences. She really did feel as though she had a friend. They knew each other's histories now.

After she left, he thought back on what she'd told him, and marveled at the strength of the human spirit, in the worst possible circumstances of loss and deprivation, and how remarkable it was that she had survived. She was a brave woman, and he felt sure that there was more she hadn't told him. He had secrets of his own. There were places in his heart where no one would ever go again.

Chapter 11

Allegra worked hard for Henry, and enjoyed every minute of it. The tasks she performed for him were varied, and she learned a great deal about his music, how he created, what inspired him, the incredible discipline he had. Sometimes he worked straight through the night without stopping, and the creative forces in him fueled him. She came to understand too that the losses and sorrows he'd had in his life, like the loss of contact with his children, somehow transformed into the music he created. She agreed with Carly's initial assessment that he was a genius. She loved learning from him, and didn't mind working hard for him, nor the long hours.

Allegra didn't work as late or as much as Henry did, but she was always willing to stay late if he asked her to or gave her extra projects at the last minute. It felt like an honor to be part of his creative process, and to make life easier for him with the things she did. He said she was the most organized person he'd ever met.

She moved two weeks after she came to work for him, having

found a furnished apartment she liked in West Hollywood. It was in a small, quaint, Spanish-style building. The furniture was vintage with a nice look to it. The apartment was neat and cozy, and there was a pool she rarely got a chance to use. But on the occasional weekends Henry didn't ask her to work on something that came up at the last minute, she enjoyed being in her apartment alone. He was so intense with his constant activity that sometimes she loved having time to herself to do absolutely nothing, and just be lazy in her apartment. It didn't happen often, which made time to herself even more precious. She used the time to read and even did some writing.

Henry was constantly in motion, constantly creating, always working on something new, and she handled all the details around him, which freed him up to do his work. When Jordan came to collaborate with him, he marveled at everything Allegra did, and couldn't keep his eyes off her. And Henry's famous short-fused temper had never surfaced in the time she worked for him. Like all creative people, he had his moody days and his quirks, but on the whole she found him surprisingly reasonable, easy to work for, and always kind to her.

She called Pippa in New York from time to time and told her about Henry. Pippa was glad for her that she had left New York and taken the job in L.A. Allegra was thriving, with a job she loved, working for a man who was teaching her a great deal, and enriching her life with everything he exposed her to. Allegra had no regrets about leaving New York. She felt as though she could breathe again.

She never heard from Shep, and still worried about him. She wasn't even sure she'd know if something happened to him since she was no longer listed as his next of kin, and his parents would never

JOY

contact her since they didn't know they'd been married. She tried not to think about it. Her divorce papers arrived at the end of the year, right before Christmas. And even though she knew about them, it was a shock. It was like an eraser wiping clean the blackboard of an important part of her life. She had loved him for eight years, a third of her life. For years, he had been her only friend. She sat and stared at the papers when she got them, and could remember every important moment between herself and Shep. She wondered if he could too, or if he had banished her from his mind as well as his heart. He had said that he was leaving her to protect her from the damage he could do to her. But if he had loved her, she thought he would have left the army and tried to get the help he needed. Instead he went back for more, and must be irreparably destroyed by now. It was a tragic loss for them both. But with time, and her new life in L.A., she was slowly recovering from the blow and the loss. Getting the official papers set her back again.

She stayed in bed for the entire weekend after she got the divorce papers and didn't speak to anyone. She didn't have any friends in L.A. Henry never gave her enough time off to meet people, or make friends, or find a man. Her job for him was all-consuming, but she loved it, so she didn't mind. And she loved how protective he was, like a guardian angel, always watching over her, guiding her, teaching her, and advising her.

When she worked particularly late, he invited her to stay for dinner, and Louise served them on trays in the library, or at the dining table when they weren't too rushed to get back to work. Sometimes they ate sandwiches in the studio, so he could continue listening to soundtracks while she watched, and he let her listen too.

When he was composing the score for a film, he watched it normally at first, then without sound to concentrate on the actors' facial expressions, then he listened to the dialogue without the images, to hear the inflections of their voices. Then he read the script and made notes. And then, finally, he began to write the music, and it flowed. He would stay with it all through the night if he had to, to capture what he heard in his head. It was the music of his soul.

Allegra had learned not to interrupt him. She was just there, in the background, if he needed anything, or wanted her to listen to some part of it. She was never lonely while she worked for him. She didn't have time to be. After a year of being constantly at his side, she had perfect instincts for whatever he might want from her, and she anticipated his every need.

She had been in his employ for a year when he had to go to England to meet with a producer. He had mentioned it when he hired her, but this was the first time he had asked her to travel with him. He was planning to go to London for a week to discuss a film they wanted him to do the score for, and he was going to Paris for a few days after that. He asked Allegra to go with him to assist him on the trip.

She had never been to Europe, and she hesitated. Henry was insistent about it, he said he needed her there as an assistant. He was adamant that he wanted her to go with him. It was just an extension of everything she did for him in L.A., and he expected her to be there. Travel had originally been part of the job description when he hired her. She was having a hard time getting out of it, she had used every excuse she could think of, and he wouldn't let her off the hook. He finally realized that she was scared.

Joy

"Why don't you want to go to London, Allegra?" he asked her late one night, in the studio, while they shared a plate of sandwiches Louise had left for them. Louise had gotten used to Allegra in the past year, and approved of how devoted she was to him. She always told him what a nice girl Allegra was, and he agreed.

"I don't know. I've never been that far away before. Maybe it has to do with never having anyone to protect me for so long. I was always having to face something new by myself." He hadn't thought of that. "Sometimes new things or being far from home scares me." She was always open and honest with him.

"But you won't be alone this time. I'll be there to protect you. And nothing bad is going to happen to you on the trip. You'll be doing all the same things to help me that you do here. I wouldn't let anything happen to you." She was afraid that she sounded like a little kid when she admitted her fear to him. She felt foolish, but she was always honest with him about her own failings, or anything she'd done wrong, which didn't happen often. But she didn't hide her mistakes from him. It was an endearing quality she had, among many. She was unfailingly honest. It touched him that she had admitted to him that she was scared.

The only thing she had never told him was about Shep and the divorce. He didn't know she'd been married. It was too personal and too painful. But she'd been candid with him about her unhappy childhood.

"Maybe I'm afraid to run into my mother in London. I really don't want to see her."

"You're not a child, Allegra. She can't hurt you anymore." He had long understood that her mother's rejection was the most devastating thing that had ever happened to her, and that she had struggled to understand it all her life.

"I know. It's stupid really. I had lunch with her before I left New York. She was perfectly pleasant. She was every time I ever saw her. She just acted like I was someone else's child. It was as though I didn't even exist. It never dawned on her that losing my grandmother mattered to me, even though we weren't close. My mother gave me my grandmother's little ruby heart pin I wear sometimes. But Mariette was *her* mother. It was as though she didn't even consider me related to her, as though I wasn't good enough to be part of her family. She didn't want me, so I never existed in her eyes. She didn't hate me. She didn't care about me enough to hate me, that would have required some form of emotion. And my father never cared enough to stick around. I was a duty visit he made for a few hours once every eighteen months or two years."

"They were terrible people," he said, deeply moved. All her life she had been the child that no one loved, and no one protected. He didn't know it, but she had then become the wife that her husband rejected and abandoned. Although with Shep it was more complicated, and she understood that. He had left her because he loved her. It was about how damaged he was, and how he had nearly killed her twice and was afraid it would happen again. He had no control over his night terrors and the demons lurking inside him that he had acquired in Iraq. But the final result was that, just like her parents, he had rejected her, abandoned her, and left her alone. It still felt too fresh to discuss with anyone. And in some remote part of her, she had still hoped that she would hear from him again some-

Joy

day. The divorce papers dashed those hopes, and confirmed that he was out of her life forever and wanted it that way.

"You don't have to see your mother while we're in London," Henry reminded her. "You'll be too busy anyway."

"I don't want to run into her on the street. I don't want to see her again. It brings back too many memories. Every time I've seen her, it takes me right back to the day she left and never said goodbye, and I spent the day terrified, hugging my bear, waiting for my father to tell me what he was going to do with me. It's too hard to see her."

"Then don't," he said simply. "Allegra the child isn't going to London. Allegra the grown-up is going, to assist me with my work." But he could only guess how deep the wounds were, and how far they went. Being abandoned by her mother had been a mortal blow to a child of six.

"I feel stupid even saying those things to you," she said, embarrassed. "I'll think about it," she said before a weekend. On Monday, she came back to work looking resolute. She looked as though she was agreeing to go to the guillotine when she told him in a voice raw with emotion that she would join him on the trip.

"I'm sorry I made a fuss about it."

"I'm glad you're going. That's all that matters. You need to put those ghosts to rest. And selfishly speaking, it will be wonderful for me and make everything easier. I promise to protect you," he said solemnly, and she smiled and went to her office, to start getting things organized for the trip. She had gotten a passport when she took the job, at Henry's suggestion.

Jordan Allen came by that afternoon. He always stopped in her office to talk to her. She thought he had an odd relationship with Henry, part hero worship and part envy.

"So you're going with him?" he said in a snide way she didn't like. It made it sound like she was taking advantage of Henry, which was the last thing she wanted to do. Jordan always put a spin on things. "London is a cool city. I'm sure he'll take you to all the best restaurants and parties." He sounded jealous when he said it, although he had a full life of his own.

"We're going to be working," she reminded him.

"He'll take some time off. He'll want to impress you," he said, and she looked at him, annoyed.

"That's not the kind of relationship we have. He's my boss." She made it sound like a sacred word, and Jordan laughed.

"Stranger things have happened when a boss takes his assistant on a trip. I'd want to impress you if you were going to London with me."

"Don't be ridiculous," she snapped at him. He was so much younger than Henry that she had no problem putting him in his place. "That's who you are, *not* who he is." He was trying to make her feel dirty and guilty and he hadn't succeeded. She knew Jordan and his reputation for chasing anything in a skirt. "Henry is a gentleman," she reminded him.

"He's a man, Allegra. And take a look in the mirror. Any man with eyes in his head would make a play for you. He's only human." It was the one part of Henry's life she didn't know about. He never discussed women with her. But Louise had told her several times that there hadn't been a serious woman, or even a lightweight one, in his life in years. He'd been too badly wounded by his ex-wife, his

Joy

only wife, to ever marry again, which Allegra always reminded Louise was an area that didn't concern her. She was there to assist him, and at best they were friends. He had never made overtures to her in the past year, and she was sure he wasn't about to start now, just because they were on a trip. She had booked their two separate rooms herself at Claridge's. She had a room and he had a suite, his usual one. He went to London at least once a year, and sometimes more often, if he had a project there.

"Wait and see. It'll happen one of these days," Jordan said with his usual arrogance, trying to make her uncomfortable. She was nervous enough, without adding to it that Henry was going to make advances to her while they were away. Jordan might have done it, as he intimated, but Henry never would. That was one part of the trip she wasn't worried about, and she was feeling better about the rest. Talking to Henry openly about it made it all seem less scary. She had now reached the stage of trying to figure out what clothes to pack, which Henry considered a good sign. She was checking the weather forecasts daily in order to decide.

When the day finally arrived, Henry picked her up at her apartment on the way to the airport. She had two big suitcases with her, which surprised him, but he didn't comment. He didn't want to make her nervous. She apologized as soon as she got into the car. Fortunately, he'd brought the van they usually used to buy groceries for the house.

"I read two conflicting weather reports. One said it was going to be unseasonably warm, the other said it would be rainy and chilly, so I brought everything for both," she said, and he laughed. They didn't need to worry, they were both traveling first class. He had asked her to book the flight that way in case he wanted to work with her on the eleven-hour trip. So she was fully prepared to do whatever he needed, or to leave him alone if he wanted to sleep, watch a film, or listen to music.

She quietly read a book after the plane took off, and they didn't speak until lunch was served. It was an elaborate meal, and he drank wine with lunch. She didn't. She considered herself "on duty" and wanted to be alert if he needed her. They both watched movies after that, and then they both slept for the remainder of the trip. They were arriving at six A.M. local time, which gave them time to get to the hotel, shower and change, and be ready for their morning meeting, refreshed after a decent night's sleep on the plane. It was a long flight but the timing worked well.

Claridge's had sent a car for them, and Allegra's eyes were wide as they drove into the city, past several famous monuments. London was a busy, bustling city, with a combination of history and modernism. The driver took them past Buckingham Palace at Henry's request, and Allegra was instantly excited and whispered to him.

"You were right. I'm glad I came." She loved the elegant, old-fashioned hotel, and was delighted with her room, decorated in bright flowered chintzes. It was the most exciting adventure of her life, and she was beaming when she went to Henry's suite for the meeting. She was wearing a very chic black linen suit, and looked elegant and professional, as well as young and beautiful. Henry smiled when he saw her.

"I'm very glad you're here with me, Allegra," he said. She had ordered a full spread of coffee, tea, and pastries for the meeting. There were four of them when the producer and his team arrived, six including Allegra and Henry. She listened quietly and didn't make any comments. They were desperate to convince Henry to work on three films with them, and they tried to make it as appealing as possible. He wasn't sure he wanted to spend as much time in London as they wanted and didn't want to agree to more than one or two of their projects. Allegra enjoyed listening to the exchange, and after the lengthy meeting, he told her he was taking her to lunch.

He took her to Rules, which he said was the oldest restaurant in London, and after that, he was sending her out with the car to see the sights and do some shopping, in optimal conditions. He was going to stay at the hotel to work but said he didn't need her.

"And we're having dinner at Harry's Bar tonight, I'm a member. You should wear something a little dressy." She was startled by the invitation. He had never taken her out to dinner before, and now he was taking her out twice in one day.

"Are you sure?" She was a little unsure. "Don't you have friends you want to see?" she asked him.

"Actually, no. I want you to have a good time in London," he said, smiling at her. "We have another meeting tomorrow morning, and then I'm sending you to the Tate Modern Museum, and after that to the Tower of London, to see the Crown Jewels. Do you like the theater?" he asked her, and she nodded. "Why don't you get us tickets for tomorrow night? We might as well have some fun while we're here." He was like the father she'd never had, spoiling her.

"Shouldn't I be working?" she asked him.

"When I want you to, I'll tell you. The rest of the time you can play tourist." His suggestions were exciting and generous, and he was emphatic about wanting her to enjoy the trip.

After lunch, the driver dropped Henry off at the hotel and took Allegra to Harrods. She had only brought one simple black dress in case she needed it, and she bought a dressier black-and-white silk dress with a matching jacket, inspired by Chanel but at a better price point, to wear to dinner that night.

She looked very chic when Henry met her in the lobby in time for dinner.

"How was your tour?" he asked her, looking very fatherly and proud of her.

"Very successful." She had bought another dress too, and loved seeing the Crown Jewels at the Tower of London. She'd ordered the theater tickets he had requested. He was courting her and he didn't even know it, while telling himself he was being paternal and protective, and she deserved to be spoiled for once in her life. He wanted good things to happen to her, and for her first trip to Europe to be a smash hit.

She loved Harry's Bar, and the delicate Italian food. The crowd was very chic and very dressy. The women were wearing cocktail dresses and the men dark blue suits, as was Henry, with an impeccable white shirt and navy tie, and for an instant she remembered Jordan's insinuations about the trip, and she brushed them aside. Henry was just being kind to her and she was grateful, and he was enjoying her company. The thirty-eight-year age difference didn't bother either of them. It seemed appropriate for boss and assistant.

"If I were younger, I'd take you to Annabel's," he said to her on the

Joy

way back to the hotel. "I'm a member there too. I keep up my London memberships for when I come here. I don't even know what people dance to these days," he said, laughing. "Maybe my music." And she laughed too. They'd had an easy, fun evening, and he told her about studying music at Juilliard in New York, and a year at the conservatory in Paris. His mother had been a piano teacher and his father was first violinist at the Metropolitan Opera. His entire youth had been steeped in music, which had been his passion all his life. But he had never become truly successful until he went to L.A. and got into films. He still loved classical music, but the composing he did now was his life. He was sad that his parents hadn't lived long enough to see his success. And like Allegra, Henry was an only child. He said that his parents had been wonderful to him, but very demanding about his music. They wanted him to be a concert pianist, and he almost had been. L.A. had changed all that.

He had met his ex-wife as soon as he got to L.A., she was an ingénue. He said it was a dream that turned into a disaster. She was supportive in the beginning. And then she had taken full advantage of him once he was successful, and eventually left him for a producer he knew who was more successful. It all happened so long ago that he wasn't bitter when he talked about it. His anger had cooled over the years, but he said he'd never forgive her for cutting him out of his children's lives. It was the first time Henry had talked to Allegra about his childhood. She understood his discipline now, after years and years of an education in classical music, with two hard-driving parents who were musicians, and hours of practicing every day. He had been able to enjoy none of the normal childhood pursuits, not even friends. He had to practice.

"I really wanted to play baseball like all the other kids. I felt persecuted until I was about fifteen, and then took my music seriously myself. My music is everything to me. Discipline is a good thing to have in life," he said. "Like you, Allegra. You're very disciplined too. It makes life easier."

They were back at the hotel by then, and he walked her to her room.

"Thank you for dinner," she said warmly. "I had an incredible day, thanks to you." He didn't want her to have another trauma in her life. And the time they spent together gave him the opportunity to tell her about his childhood and youth and his passion for his work.

"You deserve good times now, Allegra. Lots of them. Easy, happy days, surrounded by people who care about you, and protect you."

"Working for you is easy and happy. That's all I need." She was the most undemanding woman he'd ever known, and he enjoyed being with her, more than he had realized. He had loved being out with her that night. She was a beautiful young woman, with her long red hair straight down her back and her big green eyes. She didn't normally wear makeup at work, but she had worn a little that night. It made her eyes look even bigger, and more green. "See you at the meeting tomorrow morning," she said to him, and he left her as she walked into her room and he headed down the long hall to where the big suites were. Her room was more modest but very pretty. Everything about the trip had been perfect so far.

The rest of the trip was filled with meetings, lunches, dinners, and a play they both enjoyed. It felt more like a honeymoon than a business trip to Allegra, but she didn't say that to Henry. It seemed inappropriate to express it. She felt very spoiled. And she had visited all

Joy

the high spots on his list of tourist sites to visit. After being so reluctant to come, now she hated to see it end. She had seen another side of Henry, a more relaxed side. He spoke about his boyhood and his parents, his marriage and his children more openly with her, and they grew closer as a result. He knew everything about her, and she finally told him about Shep one night at dinner. He felt sorry for her. It had been one more abandonment she didn't need. But she spoke about it calmly. It had been fifteen months since Shep left, and she was able to talk about it now. It was why she had had no interest in dating since she'd gotten to Los Angeles. She hadn't been ready, and couldn't face another disappointment. She had thrown herself into her work instead. Henry said he had felt that way after his divorce too. He was deeply sympathetic about Shep and understood the crushing blow it had been.

On her last day in London, Allegra faced a dilemma. She sat in her room with some time to spare, contemplating what to do before meeting Henry for lunch, and a few last errands. She was trying to decide whether or not to call her mother. It had gnawed at her since she arrived. She hadn't planned to, but every day she wondered if she should, if it would be different, if it would be wrong to leave without calling her, or rude. She didn't owe her mother anything, but somewhere in her heart was the hope that something might have changed and there would be some bond between them that her mother hadn't been ready for before, and maybe was now. And Allegra had grown up. She didn't want to be afraid of a ghost, which was what her mother had been in her life until then.

She finally decided to call her, and told herself she had nothing to lose, and her mother could no longer hurt her. She held her breath and dialed the number. A female voice answered and asked Allegra to hold for a moment. It took several moments for her mother to come on the line. She sounded hesitant and cautious.

"Is something wrong, Allegra?" Isabelle asked her in a chilly voice.

"No, not at all. I'm in London for work, and I just thought I'd call to say hello." It seemed pathetic that she needed an excuse, but that was the relationship they had, in fact, none. Isabelle sounded immediately relieved. She'd been afraid Allegra wanted something.

"How nice of you to call," she said in a voice she would have used with a bare acquaintance. Allegra had become the daughter who simply refused to disappear entirely, and turned up every few years, by accident, whether one wanted to hear from her or not. And Isabelle didn't. "I'm leaving on a trip tomorrow, and I'm absolutely swamped. What sort of job brought you to London?"

"I'm the personal assistant to a composer. I live in L.A. now. He works in film." Allegra wanted it to sound important, and Henry was, and she hated that she still wanted to impress her mother, as though that would make a difference. It didn't. But she knew that she herself wasn't enough, and never had been.

"How nice for you," Isabelle said vaguely. "I'm so sorry to be so busy today. Have a wonderful stay."

"I'm leaving tomorrow too. We're going to Paris. Have a good trip," she said to her mother in a cooler voice. Isabelle's message was clear: Go Away. And disappear once and for all for God's sake.

"You too," Isabelle said, they both hung up and Allegra stared at the phone, wondering why she'd called her, but she knew. Because she wanted Isabelle to love her, and she never had, and still didn't, and never would. Allegra felt like a fool for calling. But she would

Joy

have felt worse if she hadn't. It finally hit her as she sat there. She didn't need Isabelle anymore. She didn't need to ever call her again. There was nothing left to say or hope for. The little girl clinging to the teddy bear named George had grown up, and she didn't need her mother anymore.

She was smiling when she met Henry in the lobby to go to lunch.

"I called my mother," she said quietly in the car, and he looked worried, fearing another injury to Allegra, and some form of rejection.

"How was it?"

"A nonevent. She was busy. So am I. I don't need her anymore," she said with a sigh. "And quite amazingly, I don't care. I don't think I'll ever call her again," she said, looking out the window, as Henry watched her and was relieved to see that she looked fine. She was smiling with a look of liberation on her face. She was free of her mother at last. It was finally over.

Chapter 12

Their three days in Paris, after London, were magical. Allegra had seen photographs and read books about Paris for years. She'd even taken two semesters of French literature in college, but nothing had prepared her for the sheer beauty of the city, and the feeling she got just walking down the streets, transported by the charm of it. Henry only had one meeting there, with a French film producer. They spent the rest of the time admiring the architecture, the monuments, the gardens, the parks, and looking at the sky, bathing in the light, which had a golden glow like no other place she'd been. It didn't get dark till ten o'clock at night. Allegra was mesmerized by all of it, and Henry loved sharing it with her. It had been his favorite city ever since he'd first been there as a young boy with his parents. And he had lived there for a year when he was at the conservatory. He knew the city perfectly.

Watching Allegra drink it all in was a special kind of joy for him. They sat at open-air cafés, walked along the Seine, watched children play in the Jardins du Luxembourg and ride the carousel near the Eiffel Tower. Every moment created a special memory she knew she would remember forever.

She had booked them into The Ritz in Paris, which was rich in history as well. They spent a morning at the Louvre and the Jeu de Paume. And wherever they went, mostly on foot, Allegra was overwhelmed by what she was seeing. Henry's suite at the illustrious hotel was palatial and the service was extraordinary. They bought crepes from street vendors, ate at bistros on the Left Bank, explored Saint-Germain-des-Prés, and walked past all the elegant shops on the Faubourg Saint-Honoré. They walked from the Place de la Concorde, the length of the Champs-Élysées to the Arc de Triomphe, with the largest French flag she'd ever seen fluttering in the breeze under the arch. The days and nights were warm. The weather was perfect, and when they got back to the hotel, on their second night there, when he said good night to her in front of her room, next to his, he kissed her, and it didn't shock her. It seemed entirely normal and what was meant to happen. They lingered in the doorway to her room, and he followed her inside and kissed her again. Her bedroom looked like a miniature of Marie Antoinette's, with heavy satin drapes in pale blue brocade, and an enormous bed with an antique headboard upholstered in the same sky-blue satin.

Henry didn't know what to say to her, he hadn't even realized how badly he wanted her, or how much he had come to love her. It all felt natural to both of them, as their clothes slipped away and they wound up in her enormous bed, making love as though they had waited a lifetime to find each other. Their passion seemed limitless in the beautiful setting, and afterward they lay in each other's arms, and he looked at her. She was like a jewel that had fallen into his hands, and he had no idea how he'd been lucky enough to find her by chance. The years between them melted away. She made him feel young again, and he made her feel like a woman, safe in his arms, where nothing could harm her. Everything that he felt for her was like a shield around her, and she kissed him gently on the lips, as he held her.

"Am I dreaming?" he whispered.

"Maybe we both are," she answered him, and lay back on the bed, her long, slim, graceful body like a dancer resting after a tour de force, as he gently caressed her, and aroused her again. She infused strength into his body and life into his soul. She gave him hope again that love did exist, that there was someone as worth loving as she was. All her love that had been pent up and unspent for years suddenly washed over him, and carried them both away. She filled him with feelings he'd long forgotten, and many he'd never felt before. He couldn't imagine his life without her anymore, and it had culminated in this exquisite moment.

There was an unexpected equality between them. They needed each other in just the right ways. There was no desperation to it. It was a peaceful sensation, like floating, as she smiled at him. It felt as though it had been meant to happen, at just this time, in that moment, in a city she could never have imagined. She wanted to come back here with him again and again, to make it theirs.

They lay awake talking and making love until the sun came up, and then they finally slept. He curled his long body around her and held her. They fit together perfectly. They could hear birds cooing as they fell asleep, and when she woke up hours later, he was still holding her. She turned around so she could look at him, and he smiled.

"I think I died and went to heaven last night. If this is a dream, don't wake me up," he said softly.

"Did you mean for this to happen?" she asked him innocently.

"Never. I didn't think I could be this lucky. I'm an old man compared to you, Allegra. How could you want me?" She had never wanted anyone so much in her life, or loved anyone as much. Every pain she had lived through seemed worth it now, if it had led her to him. She would have gone through fire for him. It didn't matter to her how old or how young either of them was. What they shared was ageless and timeless. "People will be shocked by us," he reminded her.

"I don't care," she said, rolling over on her back, and she smiled up at him, as he rested on one elbow, gazing at her in admiration and amazement.

"You're the most beautiful woman I've ever seen." He made her feel that way. It was all new to her. Everything that had come before in her life seemed like child's play now, getting her ready for him. They got out of bed and peeked out the window together. The Place Vendôme was filled with sunlight, and there was a perfect blue sky above it.

They ordered breakfast and ate in the hotel's pink bathrobes, took a bath together, and went out for a walk. She wanted to walk all over Paris with him, and be with him in the time they had left, to celebrate the miracle they'd discovered. She had no idea what they would do now, or what would happen next. All that mattered was

Joy

the perfect time they were sharing. They sat down next to each other on a bench in the Tuileries gardens under the Wedgwood blue sky and he kissed her.

"I'll race you back to the hotel if you do that again," she teased him, and he laughed. It reminded him of how young she was. He was enjoying everything about her thoroughly and marveled that she didn't care about the thirty-eight years between them. They felt like they were the same age. "I think we should stay here forever," she said, as she leaned against him. But there was no time limit to what they were sharing.

"I want to wake up with you every day," he said. "You can stay with me. We're together all the time anyway. No one will notice the difference. And we don't owe anyone any explanations. We have no parents, you have no children, mine don't see me. We're both free people."

"What about Louise? Won't she be shocked?" she reminded him with a smile about his faithful housekeeper.

"If she is, she'll get over it. I think she'll be happy for me, and she loves you." They talked about it as they walked back to the hotel, holding hands. There were other couples strolling as they were. They saw another couple kissing and they smiled. They were part of a special club now, of lovers in Paris. It was the perfect city for it. They spent the night in his room that night, which was even grander than hers. He had introduced her to a whole new world, where for the first time in her life, she felt welcome and loved, and protected by a remarkable man. He filled her life with joy.

* * *

Their idyll in Paris went too quickly, and they were still wrapped in the magic of it as they boarded their flight to Los Angeles. It felt strange to be going back now. They slept most of the way home, and she spent the night with him in Bel Air when they arrived. He put her suitcases in the guest room next to his bedroom, and told her she could use it as a dressing room. They went downstairs to breakfast in the morning, and Louise didn't say a word after she took their breakfast orders. She was smiling. And by eight o'clock they were in his studio together, ready to work. It had been a fabulous vacation and the beginning of a new life together.

"I miss Paris," she said, as she put her arms around him, and he kissed her. He had an appointment with Jordan that morning. Allegra stayed in her office. She didn't want to see Jordan, or his sly looks if he guessed that something had happened between them. He would cheapen it somehow. When he arrived, he asked Henry how Europe was, and he answered with a serious expression.

"Very productive," he said, and then they went to work. Allegra was upstairs unpacking when Jordan left.

She never stayed at her apartment in West Hollywood again, and they moved the rest of her clothes to Bel Air that first weekend. She had enough closet space in his guest room. They were both surprised by how normal it felt to be living together. It had taken a year for their love to erupt like a volcano, and only a few days to get used to sharing his bedroom. He felt like he had been waiting for her for years. And she felt the same way.

She accompanied him to the premiere of one of his films shortly after she moved in. She walked on the red carpet with him, keeping

JOY

a little distance from him so the photographers would have access to him, but he pulled her closer and tucked her hand into his arm.

"That's where you belong now," he whispered to her, and she smiled at him. They were photographed together, and Jordan commented on it at his next meeting with Henry.

"Are you dating Allegra now?" he asked him casually, and Henry looked surprised. It was such a small word for what they felt for each other. It seemed unworthy of her. Henry didn't deign to answer. Allegra deserved so much more. He broached the subject with her that night.

"We should probably wait a reasonable amount of time and do it right," he said to her. "I want to marry you, Allegra. Otherwise, people will talk, and I don't like the kind of things they say in this town. Everything is fleeting and transitory. How do you feel about it?"

"Like the luckiest woman in the world. You won't get tired of me?" she asked him with a worried look, and he smiled.

"I might, in thirty or forty years. We can talk about it then."

They married six months later in a private ceremony, performed by a judge who was a friend of Henry's. They wanted to avoid the press. Pippa flew to L.A. to be Allegra's only witness at the actual ceremony. They spent their honeymoon in Paris, and gave a reception for a hundred of Henry's friends after their honeymoon. It was a joyful affair.

Paris was as beautiful in winter as it had been in summer. It snowed while they were there, and the snow looked like lace on the streetlamps and the statues, and dusted the trees like spun sugar on a wedding cake. They spent two weeks there, going to all their favorite places. He had meetings in London afterward. She was still his assistant, which some people found odd, but it didn't bother them, they loved working together. Allegra had called Carly Forrest to tell her they were getting married, and she laughed.

"I thought it would be a good match. But I didn't realize the job would be permanent. You're the first assistant he's had who didn't quit. He wore them all out." But Allegra's energy matched his. And she loved him. Carly sent them a silver tray with their initials on it. It was their first wedding gift of many. The gossipmongers commented on their age difference, but their friends were happy for them. They complemented each other in the best possible ways.

People envied Allegra and Henry when they saw them together. It was obvious how much they loved each other. And despite the age difference, they didn't look foolish together. It looked and felt right, with mutual admiration and respect.

He won another Oscar the year after they were married. And he thanked her in his brief speech, for the limitless love and joy she gave him. He referred to her as his extraordinary wife.

They talked about having a baby and decided not to. Henry thought it wouldn't be fair to the child to have a father so old, and he admitted that he wanted Allegra to himself. She agreed with him, although she liked the idea of having his child. But her own childhood had been so traumatic that she couldn't imagine bringing children into the world, and risk damaging them in some way. She wanted to take care of him now, and didn't want to share him either. Their bond to

Joy

each other was so close and so tight there was no room in it for anyone else, not even a child of their own. They were happy as they were.

Henry did the scores for two more films with Jordan, who told him how lucky he was to have Allegra. Henry was his idol, his hero, and he admitted readily that he was jealous of him, for many things, and especially the wife he had. But he conceded that Henry deserved her, and he had never seen two people more in love.

Allegra and Henry went to Paris every year, to honor their first trip there. It was where everything had started and when they had both realized that they were in love.

It was an excellent excuse to come to Paris. London never had the same meaning to them, or the same magic. And when she went to London with him, once they were married, she didn't call her mother, and she never called her again. It had been the best decision she'd ever made. She had no regrets about letting her go. Isabelle never called her either. She never had. And she had finally gotten the distance she wanted from Allegra. She wanted no relationship with her, and no reminders of the past. Nor did Allegra. She had Henry now. He was all she needed. In all the years they shared, she felt happy and safe.

Henry gave Allegra a surprise party for her thirtieth birthday. He was sixty-eight years old, vital and strong and healthy. She took good care of him, and he looked younger than when she'd married him. They celebrated their fifth anniversary that year, and spent it in Paris at the Ritz, as always, in the same suite as before.

He hadn't slowed down and worked just as hard. He still worked straight through the night sometimes and was just as intense about his music and scores. She worked with him as diligently as she had when she first came to work for him. She was as tireless as he was, and they were an efficient, energetic, synchronized team. She knew everything there was to know about his business and listened to every note of every score with him. She loved the music he composed.

Jordan had become famous by then, and came to Allegra's surprise thirtieth birthday with a well-known actress he was dating. He was forty-one by then, and marriage was still the farthest thing from his mind. There was always a younger, more beautiful woman just around the corner that he was hoping to meet. His conquests were legendary, and the women were all celebrities now, which he felt enhanced his image. He was known to go out with the most beautiful women in Hollywood, though never for long. The longevity of his relationships had never been important to him. He always said he wasn't as lucky as Henry, to have met the love of his life. He claimed he was still looking but hadn't found her yet. And Henry had won the prize.

Allegra wanted Henry to reach out to his children, and see if he could connect with them now, with her support. But he never did it. He said it was too late. They were strangers to each other, related

Joy

only by blood, which wasn't enough of a connection. His ex-wife had succeeded in separating them forever, which Allegra regretted for him, but she couldn't convince him otherwise. He was entirely satisfied with her, and didn't need anyone else in the inner circle of their life together. They had friends, but the only person he was truly close to, and who knew him intimately, was Allegra. It was enough for him, and for both of them.

They lived together, worked together, traveled together. They hadn't spent a night apart since they married. She called Pippa from time to time and stayed in touch with her. She was genuinely happy for Allegra. Pippa always wondered what had happened to Shep, but she didn't dare ask. Allegra didn't know, and never tried to find out. She had no idea if he was still alive or not. He had receded into the mists of her past. And it seemed best to leave it that way. There were too many old ghosts there that she didn't want to meet again, or even know about, like her mother. She was finally truly gone, which was a relief to them both.

Henry always said that he had never known anyone who had experienced so much trauma and heartbreak and come out of it whole, as she had. He said it to Pippa at their wedding reception, which she flew to L.A. for. She didn't know most of it, but she agreed, just based on what she knew, and what Allegra had shared with her in New York. Pippa and Henry liked each other, and she loved him for being so good to Allegra.

Allegra's bond with Henry grew stronger with each passing year. Loving him and being loved by him made up for all the pain she'd ever been through. He was her reward for surviving. And the past no longer mattered at all.

Chapter 13

They'd been married for seven years when Henry turned seventy. He was as vital as ever, worked on just as many movies, and was constantly in demand. People who worked with him saw no difference in him, but Allegra began to see subtle changes in him after his birthday. He tired more easily, although he would never admit it to her or himself. She protected him as best she could from his demanding lifestyle and still-booming career. He was scoring more movies than ever before, and traveling even more than he used to. He had worked on two movies in France and one in England in the past year, in addition to the American ones.

Allegra went on all his trips with him and kept his life organized. She was glad they had never had children. They wouldn't have been able to spend enough time with them. Henry lived the lives of ten people, with the strength of twenty men. He had the vitality of a forty-year-old, and looked sixty at most. She saw to it that he ate the right food and took care of his health.

She was shocked when a bad cold he caught on a flight from London turned into bronchitis, and then pneumonia. He usually never got sick.

"You're working too hard," she chided him gently. "You can't run all over Europe and juggle three films in L.A. at the same time. No one can do that." But he had been for a long time. Nothing slowed him down, and his fresh new ideas for scores were the envy of everyone in the business. He was nominated for another Oscar but didn't win that time.

Once he had pneumonia, the doctor told him he had to slow down, and Henry knew he did too. It was another three weeks before Allegra discovered why he was so sick. It wasn't the travel, or not entirely. Henry finally confessed. The doctor told him it was unfair not to tell Allegra. He had known for five months that he had a rare form of stomach cancer. It was considered incurable. Chemo wouldn't cure it, but it would slow it down for a while, which was the best they could hope for. Henry faced the prognosis bravely. All he wanted was to continue his work until his last breath and to spend every moment he could with Allegra. Chemotherapy would buy him a little more time, but the side effects would severely impact his quality of life. He decided it wasn't worth it. He didn't want the last months of his life to be riddled with pain and nausea. He didn't want Allegra to have that as her final memories of them. He had remained staunch and stoic. It wasn't the end yet, but the doctor shared with her that they were looking at months, not years. She would have some more time with him until he got weaker.

Allegra didn't leave Henry alone for a second after that. She was his shadow. She knew what he needed and wanted before he even

JOY

thought of it himself. She made working possible and comfortable for him, once they cured the pneumonia. But the doctor said it would happen again, as his body became less and less able to fight off infections. There were other maladies too that would plague him, as his body's defenses slowly shut down. There was still time for chemo, if Henry agreed to it, but he refused. He wanted to be fully functioning, or as close to it as possible, to the end. He was still supervising recording sessions and working in his studio until all hours. It was hard to believe he was sick. Allegra began to think the doctors had made a mistake in their diagnosis. He seemed better at times.

She and Henry went on walks together, although he tired faster now. They talked endlessly. He felt as though he had to say everything to her that he might forget later. He was braced for a very rough patch at the end, but he wasn't there yet. He wanted to fully function for as long as he was able. Allegra begged him to try the chemo. He could always stop it if he hated it and it made him too sick, but he continued to refuse. He was a noble warrior and intended to go out as one, so she'd be proud of him. He didn't want to give up what they had. It was too precious to him, and so was she. He wanted her to remember their best days, not the end.

They didn't tell anyone that Henry was sick. He didn't want to be seen that way, as diminished and weak, less than he had been before. He had incredible stamina and courage. Allegra tried to share her own strength with him so he would live longer. She prayed for a miracle but it didn't come. She had an inexhaustible supply of love for him. She would have given him her own life if she could.

* * *

They shared a thousand precious moments in his final months, and she cherished each of them like jewels to be treasured. She knew she would live from them for the rest of her life. The journey would be hard without him. Harder than everything she'd lived through before, because she had shared such intense happiness with him. But she knew she would always feel him near her. Their last days together were among the greatest gifts he ever gave her.

He worked hard until the end, and the music he composed was beautiful, with a bittersweet haunting quality to it. His final work was like an explosion of joy, the culmination of a lifetime. He dedicated it to her and called it simply "Allegra," the joyous one.

Jordan had stopped coming to see him. He had come to love Henry as best he could and couldn't bear to see him so ill. He cried like a child the last time he left. He knew he wouldn't see him again. He had no words to tell Allegra what he felt, and was bowled over by their courage. Their love sustained them and gave them strength.

Allegra was with Henry every instant of every day and night, cherishing him, loving him, feeding him, nurturing him, making him laugh when he could, talking for hours, or watching him when he slept. He took as little medication as possible for the pain. He wanted to be alert to share every moment with her, and not dull his senses or sleep his final days away.

On his last day, he got up and they took a walk in the garden. It was a beautiful summer day. There were butterflies everywhere, and a hummingbird stopped in midair to watch them. Henry pointed it out to her, and the flowers were in full bloom all around them. He seemed suddenly stronger, he talked about his boyhood, and his children, and was sorry he hadn't gotten to know them. But Allegra

Joy

had filled every space in his heart for the best seven years of his life. It was a gift they had given each other. Together they were more than either of them had ever been before. For the first time in her life, she had known that she was truly loved, and nothing could take that away. Nothing would erase it or change it or spoil it or cast a shadow on the love they had shared.

"You know," she said to Henry quietly as they walked back to the house. He had more energy than he'd had in weeks. "Few people are as lucky as we are," she said peacefully. "Most people never know a love like this. They waste their time and their lives with all the wrong ones." Allegra had done that herself, chasing her mother for years, hoping her father would come home, not to neglect her again and reject her, but to love her. She had tried to convince her grandparents to love her by making herself as small as possible, and hanging on to Shep in desperation when he was too broken to love her. She had chased all the shadows and the dreams until she met Henry, and he had given her his heart and his trust and his joy of living so gracefully, generously, and simply. She didn't have to fight for it, or beg, or convince him.

"I was so lucky I found you," he said, smiling at her, "it was a miracle. Thank God you were brave enough to come to L.A. Imagine if you hadn't. We would have missed everything."

"I was meant to be here," she said simply. "I was sent to you." Neither of them doubted it.

"And I had waited for you for years. You could have come a bit faster," he said, and laughed. His laugh was still strong, like his love for her, and his spirit.

"I was busy," she said primly, "chasing all the wrong people down all the wrong paths. They were my lesson to learn before I met you," and she had loved working with him.

"You are my lesson," he said proudly. "I learn from you every day."

They went back to their bedroom, and he lay down. He could see the garden from their bed. The windows were open and there was a soft breeze in the room. He loved seeing the vibrant colors, and he had a piece of music in his head. "I'm going to compose later," he said to her. He hadn't been to his studio in three days. He had a half-written score on his desk he wanted to finish.

She lay down next to him, and Henry laid his head on her shoulder and she gently stroked his face and his hair. He smiled, loving the feel of her fingers on his skin—they felt like angel kisses, he had once said. "I love you, Allegra," he said with a smile, and with a gentle breath he was gone, like a whisper in her heart. He hadn't said goodbye, but he didn't need to. She knew how much they loved each other. Every moment of their seven years together had been a love poem from beginning to end, a song of joy. His love had washed away all the sorrows of her past and filled her heart with happiness, enough to last for the rest of her life.

Chapter 14

The music Allegra chose for Henry's funeral was all written by him. Many of the pieces, he had written for her. All of them were filled with joy and uplifting. The music said more about him than any of the many eulogies that were spoken. Allegra sat alone in the front pew of the church. She didn't want anyone with her, or need them. She felt Henry next to her.

She wore a simple black dress he had bought her in Paris, and a hat he loved, and the music transported everyone in the church. Every seat was filled, and there were rows of people standing behind them, to honor the man and his talent. Henry was too young to go, but he had filled every moment of his life with beauty for others to enjoy. He had made everyone's life better because he had lived, especially Allegra's. He had been the healing that had come to compensate her for the past. The tidal wave of his love had washed away the cruelty of others. She knew full well how fortunate she was to have loved him and been loved by him. He was the miracle she had waited for.

Allegra had invited his children to the funeral, but they had responded that they truly didn't know him and felt awkward coming, so they didn't. She knew Henry would have understood, but she was sorry they hadn't come. It would have been a suitable gesture of respect for their father. He didn't expect them to.

She held a reception afterward at the Hotel Bel-Air. There were too many people for the house. Every famous name and face in Hollywood was there. His English producers had come and so had the French director he had worked with recently. Carly was there, out of affection and respect. Pippa flew out from New York for the service, and to be there for Allegra. Jordan came and looked devastated. He hugged Allegra and couldn't speak. She had asked him to be one of the pallbearers and he was touched and honored to be recognized as one of Henry's closest friends. Henry had liked him and understood who he was, accepted him with his weaknesses, and said he was young. Jordan had come to the funeral with the actress he was dating at the moment, and he was struck by how beautiful Allegra looked. She looked serene as she walked gracefully through the crowd at the Bel-Air and thanked people for coming, and touched a hand, or gave someone a hug. She looked as though she wasn't really there. She had worn a widow's veil with the black hat, and it made her look even more beautiful. Her looks had become more radiant and more striking over the years in the warmth of Henry's love and tender care of her. All the marks of the past had been smoothed away, the pain, the anxiety, the wounds, the deep hurts

JOY

others had inflicted on her. Henry's love had washed them away, like a perfect white stone on the beach, smoothed by the sea.

Allegra went back to the house after the reception. Henry's friends and the people he had worked with were still at the hotel, talking and drinking and laughing, and telling stories about him. He had been fierce in his youth and mellowed with time. She took off the hat and veil when she got home, changed into a plain white cotton dress, and went to sit in the garden, thinking of Henry and their last walk there, only a few days before, on his last day, in his final hour, although they didn't know it. A large blue butterfly came to rest on her hand, and she smiled at it and lifted it close to her face. It caressed her cheek and flew away, and she knew it was him. He was free now, on the wings of his music, to a better place. She already missed him, but felt the same joy whenever she thought of him. It was like a summer breeze that soothed her heart.

Allegra sat in the garden for a long time, as Louise watched her from the kitchen window, with a worried expression. She had gone to the funeral in her best black dress, and changed when she came home too.

"She's so alone now, no family, no children . . ." Louise said to Fred, the houseman who did the heavy cleaning. "What will she do?"

"She'll meet someone else. She's young. He was a lot older. She was always going to be a widow one day," he said practically. Louise looked annoyed.

"She's not like that," she snapped at him. "They really loved each other. She's a good woman." Henry had died at seventy-one. Allegra was thirty-three. And Fred was right, she was young, but she seemed much more mature than her years. She had a depth that most women her age didn't have yet. She had a lifetime ahead of her, and wasn't even halfway yet, most likely. Louise couldn't imagine her without Henry now. Neither could Allegra. She could no longer remember her life without him.

She wandered into the studio and looked at the notes on his desk of the last unfinished piece. She could read music now, he had taught her. She put one of his scores on, one of her favorites. It made her feel peaceful. She had to go through his papers, but it was still too soon. She couldn't yet. She had time. She had nothing to do now without him. She had dedicated her whole life to him for the past seven years. It seemed like an entire lifetime, not just part of it. It was the most important part.

Allegra stayed in the studio for hours, touching things, reading his notes, listening to his music. She stayed there until she went to bed. She didn't want to eat, and Louise left her alone. She would have to find her way now, and this was just the beginning. It would be a long life without him.

Henry's lawyer contacted Allegra a few days after the funeral. He had a copy of the will for her, which she wasn't interested in, but he said she had to see it. Henry had written it himself, in simple terms, and it was legally binding. He had left everything to Allegra and a generous bequest to Louise, his housekeeper. His ex-wife had made a lucky investment in the dot.com craze, and had become a rich woman. He knew his children would be taken care of by their

Joy

mother, and both had good jobs. He checked on them occasionally from a distance. And Allegra was alone now. Henry didn't have a large fortune, but she would be very comfortable for a long time, forever if she was careful and wise. The house was his most valuable possession and she could sell it one day if she needed to. There would be income from his music, even quite a lot, for the rest of her life. She didn't have a vast amount of money now, but he had left her wealthy enough to be safe, and able to do what she wanted. She didn't have to work, or worry, thanks to him. As he had with everything else, Henry had been responsible and generous with Allegra. And he had added a paragraph that said she was to go to Paris whenever she wanted to, and stay at the Ritz. It made her smile when she read it. She would do that one day, but she needed to catch her breath and get her bearings first. Henry had left an incredible void in her life, and she didn't know how to fill it.

Over the next weeks, Allegra went through all Henry's papers and notes and articles about him, the biographical data, some of which she knew. But he hadn't told her of all the awards he'd received. There were dozens of them, along with his three Oscars. She found an envelope of photographs of him with his children. They had been four and five when he got divorced. She realized that they probably had no memory of him at all. She had the photographs copied and sent to them via Henry's lawyer.

As the stack of historical data on Henry's desk grew, Allegra realized how she was going to spend her time now. She had always wanted to try her hand at writing. The time had come. Henry had always encouraged her to try it. She was going to write a book about him, and the title came to her at the same time as the idea. *Ode to Joy.* It was perfect to describe his life, with all due respect to Beethoven, who she was sure wouldn't have objected.

It was exciting to think about the project and start putting order to the material she was collecting. She pulled out old files and made copies of everything. Writing the book would give meaning and direction to her life, and honor his. In many ways, he had been the unsung hero of the more classical music world, because his work was considered commercial, because of his success.

She was sitting on the studio floor, surrounded by papers and photographs in neat piles in chronological order, when Jordan came to visit her for the first time, three weeks after Henry died. He had wanted to give her time to begin recovering before intruding on her. He still wasn't sure if it was too soon, as he walked hesitantly into the studio and saw her on the floor. She looked up at him with a pale serious face and her red hair piled on top of her head with a pencil through it. She looked painfully beautiful, but he didn't say it.

"I'm going to write a book about him," she said to Jordan, and he nodded, equally serious. It saddened him to come to the house and not find Henry there. He had filled every inch of space around him with such vibrancy. The house was so silent now without him. Jordan could easily imagine how lonely Allegra was. But she was excited about the book she was planning. Her eyes were bright when she told Jordan about it.

"You should. He would love it," Jordan said, and sat down on the floor with her. "Someone should have written one about him years

Joy

ago. He should have done it himself. He had so many great stories to tell."

"He never had time to write about them, he was too busy living them," Allegra said, and handed Jordan a photograph of Henry that made him laugh. He was on a beach somewhere, a young man fooling around with a pretty girl next to him. Jordan turned the photo over and Henry had written "Summer of Love, 1967." The girl was a Twiggy look-alike, which made Jordan smile, and Allegra had too. Henry was twenty-five at the time.

"What are you doing with yourself these days?" Jordan asked Allegra gently. He felt so sorry for her, alone now. She had lived to help Henry, and now all she had were a stack of papers and old photographs, but it made her happy to go through them. It kept him alive in her mind and daily routine.

"This," she said simply, looking around her.

"Can I take you out to dinner sometime, to get you out of the house?" he offered sincerely, as a friend. He thought Henry would want him to take care of her. Allegra wasn't as sure. Henry was wiser than that.

"Not yet. It's too soon. But thank you. I'm happy at home, going through all this stuff. It will take months to get through it all."

"Well, don't wait months to get out of here for a few hours. It would do you good," Jordan said, and she nodded.

Allegra spent the whole summer going through Henry's papers, and finding treasures to put in the book she was going to write.

Jordan dropped by to see her once a week. He brought her chocolates and pastry, some silly jokes, an occasional book to read. He always suggested lunch or dinner, but she was happy at home and didn't want to go out. She hadn't seen anyone since the funeral except Jordan, and she had to admit he was being a faithful friend. There were no inappropriate nuances, he was just concerned about her.

In September, she started the book. It filled her days and her nights, and her heart with joy, as she told Henry's story and shared his history, and she had mountains of photographs to include. She hadn't spoken to a publisher about it and hadn't tried to find an agent. She wanted to wait until the book was complete, and she guessed that it would take her a year or two, at the pace she was going. She was trying to be meticulous and historically accurate. She admitted to Jordan how much she loved writing it, when he dropped by.

"Maybe I'll try to write a novel when I finish," she said. She was enjoying writing the book about Henry immensely. She wanted to honor him, and it kept him alive while she wrote it. His energy jumped off the page and was contagious.

Allegra didn't let Jordan read it while she was working on it. She wanted it to be perfect before anyone read it, and it was still in very rough draft form. He couldn't wait to read it.

"Am I in it?" he asked hopefully.

"I don't know," she said. "I haven't gotten to that part yet. You probably should be. You did a lot of work together."

"He loved me," Jordan said, and she laughed at him. He was such a narcissist, but he had been a faithful friend since Henry died, and she appreciated it. "Speaking of which," he changed the subject, "will you go to the premiere of my new movie with me? It would do you good to get out." He made it sound like a form of therapy he was recommending to her, but she didn't feel ready to go out in public yet, to something where she'd be that visible.

"I don't think I'm up to it. Don't you have a date?"

"No one I want to be in the papers with. I'm between dates at the moment," he said, and she smiled at him.

"When is it?" She felt sorry for him sometimes. The women in his life were so transitory, and never deep enough to be real. But he liked them that way, so he was always the star.

"It's in December." Henry would be gone for six months by then. It seemed soon to her.

Jordan renewed his offer several times in the next month, and he was insistent. "It would be good pre-publicity for your book. You can tell them on the red carpet that you're writing Henry's biography," he said, and Allegra laughed at him.

"Now, that's really a stretch. You must be desperate," she said, and he smiled. He noticed that she was regaining her sense of humor recently. She and Henry had always had wry exchanges and were funny with each other. Allegra was in increasingly good spirits as she progressed with the book. She felt as though she was spending every day with Henry as she wrote the story of his life and his remarkable career in music.

Three days before the film premiere, Jordan asked her again. He still didn't have a date, and on the spur of the moment, Allegra surprised him and herself and said yes.

"But no after-parties. I don't want to go out to big social events until the year is up, and maybe never again." She couldn't imagine going to a party without Henry and didn't want to. She didn't want to play the grieving widow, or go to events without him. It wouldn't be fun anyway. "You can send me home, and go to the parties on your own," she said.

"Thank you! I want you to see the film, and you'll make me look respectable," Jordan said, elated. It wasn't a movie Henry had worked on, which would have been too emotional for Allegra.

She pulled a serious black evening gown out of her closet, and had second thoughts about going, but she'd promised and didn't want to disappoint Jordan.

On the night of the premiere, Allegra put on the dress with black satin high heels and simple diamond earrings Henry had given her, and swept her red hair up in a chic French twist. She looked simple and elegant and dignified, and she thought Henry would have approved, and wouldn't have minded her going out.

She walked down the red carpet with Jordan, as he preened for the camera as he always did. He looked movie-star-handsome in a simple Armani tuxedo, and it took a minute but then the photographers realized who she was, and respectfully asked if they could take her picture. They didn't look like a romantic couple, and Jordan told them it was her first night out. They took a portrait of the two of them, and then she stepped back and they photographed Jordan alone.

Allegra liked the movie. She left as soon as it was over, and Jordan went on to the parties. The evening had gone smoothly, she hadn't had a good time, but she hadn't had a bad time either, and Jordan was right. It felt good to dress up and get out of the house.

Joy

The next day, there was a photograph of them in the entertainment section with the caption under it: "Screenwriter Jordan Allen escorts Allegra Platt, widow of friend and composer Henry Platt, to her first evening out since her late husband's death of cancer in June." It was simple and clean and accurate and there were no innuendos. Allegra and Jordan were standing next to each other like friends, not dates. And she looked serious. Jordan was smiling.

The day after the premiere, she thanked Jordan for a nice evening and went back to work on the book. She had written straight through Thanksgiving and intended to do the same on Christmas. She didn't get a tree and didn't want one. She had her memories of Henry and the holidays they'd shared to keep her warm. Jordan went to Aspen, and she didn't hear from him until well after New Year's. He had met someone there, which kept him busy through January, while she kept writing, and the manuscript was growing. Pippa called her from time to time to check on her progress and Allegra said she was happy with it. Pippa couldn't wait to read it.

Jordan came to visit a little less frequently in January and February, with a new woman in his life, and Allegra teased him about it when she saw him.

"Don't worry. Valentine's Day will kill it," he said cheerfully. "I think she's expecting me to propose, and we know that's not going to happen." He was right, and they broke up two days later, and he resumed his weekly visits to Allegra.

In March, at the very last minute, he asked her to go to the Academy Awards with him. He was nominated again, and he wanted to attend with a serious woman, "not a cupcake," as he put it.

"Should I be flattered or offended?" Allegra asked him.

"Both. You should be more of a cupcake at your age, it would do you good. And I'd rather go with you than anyone else."

"I'll think about it," was all Allegra would say. But it seemed like a friendly gesture to go with him and support him, especially if he didn't win. Jordan had been a faithful friend to her, and had been visiting her regularly for nine months. In the end, she made the same deal with him she had for his premiere, to go to the award ceremony with him, but not the after-parties. The parties after the Oscars were always boisterous and a lot of fun. But she wasn't ready for that. She still hadn't had dinner out with him, or anyone. Henry's friends had stopped asking when she said she was going to remain in mourning for a year. But the Academy Awards were almost like a work night for anyone in the entertainment industry, and it would be a big deal for Jordan if he won. It would be nice to be there for him, rather than some ambitious starlet who barely knew him.

She wore a black satin evening gown that molded her figure and was sexier than the dress she'd worn to his premiere. But the Oscars were a big deal and she wanted to do honor to both Jordan, as her friend, and her late husband, and look beautiful. She wore her red hair down, and very high heels, and when Jordan saw her he sucked in his breath and whistled.

"Oh my God, Allegra, you look like Rita Hayworth, only better."

"Too campy?" she asked him, worried. She was out of practice, but women went all out at the Academy Awards, and so did the men. Her black evening gown was magnificent and very flattering.

"You look fantastic!" he confirmed.

Joy

They walked the red carpet and drew a lot of attention this time. It was a much more important event. Jordan was a very successful screenwriter and she was the widow of an important man. She looked beautiful, and they were a camera-worthy couple and got lots of attention from the press. Allegra felt a little conspicuous, but she focused on encouraging Jordan through the evening, and when he didn't win, she squeezed his hand and told him the third time was the charm.

"You'll win it next time," she whispered, as another screenwriter ran up on stage to collect his Oscar.

Jordan wasn't in the mood for the after-parties, and she had said she wasn't going, so he took her home, and she invited him in for a drink to cheer him up. He looked really down once they left the theater where the ceremony was held, and she poured him a scotch on the rocks when they got home, and they went to sit in the living room. Allegra hadn't used it in months, but it seemed suitable for the way they were dressed.

"You looked incredibly beautiful," Jordan said to her, as he took a big swallow of the scotch and came to sit next to her on the couch. "I feel like a total loser. Probably because I lost." He laughed at himself.

"It really is brutal having to hear the bad news in front of thousands of your peers, and millions of viewers on national TV," she sympathized. "I'd rather hear it at home in my jeans or my pajamas, if it were me," she said, and he laughed again.

"Yeah, but then I wouldn't get to show off with you on the red carpet," he said, and looked boyish. There was no denying he had charm and a certain vulnerable appeal, especially when he was down, like tonight. He touched her bare shoulder then, and looked at her, and before she knew what happened, he was kissing her, sensually, slowly, and then passionately, and she was kissing him back. Allegra was breathless when he stopped, and he ran his hands over her then, and kept kissing her as he cupped her breasts in his hands, and suddenly she didn't want him to stop. She was lonely for Henry, she had been alone for nine months, and Jordan was suddenly sexy and desirable and young, and she couldn't stop. She followed him blindly up the stairs to her bedroom at full speed, where he had her dress off in seconds, and his clothes, and before she knew what she was doing, they were making love and she forgot everything except the throbbing pulse inside her, and the magic spell he was weaving on her. It was one of the rawest, most passionate moments of her life, beyond thinking, beyond shame or conscience, and she was suddenly a young woman desperate for a man, and he was equally desperate for her. It had nothing to do with love, it was only about need and sex. They were both breathless when they stopped. She looked at him, lying on her bed, unable to believe what she'd just done. And she hadn't even had a drink. She was drunk, but on him.

"God, Jordan, what are we doing?" she whispered to him, as he touched her breast again and it responded to him immediately.

"I've wanted you since the first day I saw you, when Henry hired you. I think I fell in love with you then, but he saw you first." Allegra was shocked by what Jordan said, and she sat up on the bed. He had a spectacular body, and so did she. But hers belonged to Henry. Only Henry was no longer there. And Jordan was.

"You can't be serious," she said in response to him.

"I am. Completely. I have envied him ever since. He was my hero,

Joy

and he got the woman of my dreams. I don't even care that I didn't win tonight. I'd rather be here with you." He sounded as though he meant it, and she didn't know what to think. She had loved her husband beyond anything on earth and she had just had raw, uncontrolled, passionate sex with another man, and enjoyed it, which was even worse. She felt acutely guilty.

Minutes later, they did it again, and she hadn't even figured out how it had happened the first time. He had cast some kind of spell on her. She couldn't get enough of him, and he felt the same. Her dress lay in a heap on the floor, and her marriage and judgment with it. And for Jordan it was one of the most important moments of his life. He had been competitive with Henry Platt for all the years he knew him, and envied him everything he had, including and especially his wife. It no longer mattered that he had lost the Oscar that night. It had taken him nine years, but he had finally won Allegra. She was the prize.

Chapter 15

The morning after Allegra had sex with Jordan, she woke up at six o'clock, rolled gently off the bed, tiptoed to her bathroom, and put on a white satin robe. She couldn't even call what they'd done making love. It was pure raw, unbridled sex, of a kind she'd never had before with anyone. He was a skilled lover and she had felt and done things she'd never done before.

She was coming out of the bathroom when she saw him standing naked in her bedroom, looking at her. The healthy youthful beauty of his body was hard to ignore. And she didn't want to, but she knew she was in over her head. She had never dealt with anyone like him before. She had only slept with two men in her life, Henry and Shep, and she had married both of them. Jordan was not the kind of man one married, nor was he easy to resist.

"Don't run away," he whispered gently. "Come back to bed," and she followed him and sat on her bed. He had always wanted to be there, and now he was.

"We need to talk," Allegra said seriously. "I don't know what happened last night. I went nuts."

"I know what happened last night," Jordan said, confidently stretched out on her bed in all his naked splendor. He looked totally at ease. "I've been in love with you for nine years and I couldn't stop myself. And you can't live like a recluse forever. You're young, you need to live and get out of this house and do more of what you did last night."

"Henry's been gone for nine months. I acted like a slut," she said, mortified and feeling guilty. She felt as though she had cheated on her husband.

"Your body can't tell time, Allegra. You were married to a man nearly forty years older than you. You need to rewind the film now, and be your age, with someone closer to your age. You didn't do anything wrong."

"And then what? I'm the flavor of the month? Jordan, I know you. You've never been with a woman for longer than six weeks in your life, maybe seven. That's not who I am, or what I want."

"That's because I couldn't have you, and thought I never could. This is a game-changer. You're free now."

"I'm not free. And this isn't a game, not to me. I loved Henry. It'll be years before I want to be with someone else, maybe never. I don't want some insane fling, or to be your sex slave." He smiled.

"Excuse me, Miss Prim and Proper, *Mrs.* Proper, that was me in bed with you last night. I didn't notice any hesitation, and if there's going to be a sex slave around here, after last night it's more likely to be me."

"We need to think this thing through," she insisted. "I want to

Joy

wait another three months, until Henry's anniversary, and if you're serious, we can discuss it, and take things slowly. I'm not rushing into anything. I don't want to do anything crazy or make a terrible mistake."

"I agree with you completely," he said in a velvet tone, as he ran his fingers between her thighs and kissed her and gently laid her back on the bed. Within minutes, they were doing it again and didn't stop until he had made her come so many times she was seeing stars. When she could see clearly again, she got out of bed.

"This has to stop!" she said to him, standing next to her bed and glaring at him, and he laughed.

"Are you talking to me or yourself?" he asked her.

"Both of us," she said, but she didn't even feel guilty this time, which made it even worse. She wanted more. "Clearly, I've lost my mind."

"Maybe you've found it. Henry was right for you for the years you shared with him. But he's been gone for almost a year. You're alive. You have a right to be. You need a life, Allegra. You need to get out of this house. You're turning it into a tomb, for you. Why can't we be together? I've waited years for you. We have a right to be young and in love. It's our time now."

"I'm not so sure this is love," she said, still talking to him from several feet away. In fact, she strongly doubted it. It was nothing like what she and Henry had shared and she missed so much. Jordan wasn't the answer.

"Then let's find out. Let's have fun. Let's take this out for a spin and try it. So far, it seems pretty damn good to me. And the chemistry side of it is definitely working. I haven't had sex that many times in one night in years. I'm forty-five for chrissakes, not twenty-two. You make me feel like a kid again." He made her feel that way too. She had enjoyed it, more than she wanted to admit. That was the problem. It all felt too good. But was it right? She didn't want to rush into anything, and she already had.

"This doesn't feel real to me," she said. "I didn't sleep with Henry for a year after we met, we didn't even think of it." And it had been two years before she slept with Shep. "We jumped into this last night like two irresponsible kids."

"I've waited nine years for you," he said, and he looked like he meant it, which touched her. Maybe he was for real. He'd have to prove it. If they could stay out of bed for long enough to talk to each other.

"I'm going to take a shower," she said, "and then I'll make you breakfast." Louise was off, and they were alone in the house, which was a good thing. Allegra didn't want her to know that Jordan had spent the night, let alone what they'd done. Louise would have been shocked, justifiably. Allegra was shocked herself.

Allegra went to take a shower, letting the water pelt down on her while she tried to figure out what she was doing, and as she stood there with her eyes closed, she felt Jordan behind her, and he gently turned her around.

"You're not going to get rid of me, Allegra. I've waited too long for you. I'm in love with you. Give me a chance and I'll prove it to you." She put her arms around him then, and they made love again, in the shower. It took them another hour to get downstairs to the kitchen. He had a towel around his waist, and she was wearing her white satin robe. She made him breakfast and set it down in front of him.

Joy

She felt like she had taken a trip to the moon and had just landed back on Earth.

"Don't rush me, Jordan. I really do need time to think about it. I don't want to make a big mess with you. If this is real, we'll know," she said, and he nodded.

"I promise. I don't want to blow it with you, it's too important to me. I think Henry would be happy for us."

"I don't. I think he'd think we're both nuts," and she knew Henry had no respect for how Jordan dealt with women, with a revolving door on his bedroom.

Jordan dressed and left finally after breakfast, wearing his tuxedo from the night before, with his shirt open and his tie sticking out of his pocket. Neither he nor Allegra had the energy to make love again.

He called her that night at midnight. She was lying in bed, thinking about what they'd done, and about him, wondering if he was being honest with her, and himself.

"Can I come over?" he asked in a deep, sensual voice.

"No. The housekeeper will be here too early in the morning." She felt like a schoolteacher as she said it, scolding a little boy. He sounded disappointed. "Besides, calling at midnight is a booty call."

"You are *not* a booty call, Allegra," he said.

"I hope not. You've got some bad habits, Jordan," she said sternly, and then softened, "and some very good ones."

"Will you have dinner with me one night?" he asked her.

"Yes."

"Tomorrow?"

"Okay." When Allegra hung up, she found she was looking forward to it. More than she wanted to. She realized how lonely she had been without Henry, and Jordan had tapped into that, and she couldn't resist him. She wanted to try, to test the waters and see if he was for real or if she was just another passing fancy. She knew she wasn't ready to move on, even if she had behaved like a maniac with Jordan. His whole seduction scene had been done so well. Was it an act or was it real? Time would tell.

Their dinner the following night was perfect. He took her to a little Italian restaurant in Santa Monica with fantastic pasta. They talked like normal people and he made her laugh. It felt good to be out and to talk. She told him about her progress on the book. When he was serious, and not acting like a playboy, she always liked him. She couldn't imagine what it would be like to be together. After Henry, Jordan seemed immature to her. But no one measured up to Henry. And probably never would again.

They did wind up in bed that night after dinner, but Allegra made him leave afterward, because she knew she'd never get him out in the morning before Louise arrived. She liked to get to work early, at six. But the evening had been more normal, and so was the sex. Jordan texted her when he got home and said he loved her. She didn't know why, but she didn't believe him. It sounded more like something he knew he should say. It didn't feel real or honest. And she didn't love him. She liked him, but she wasn't in love with him. Yet. It was happening too fast.

* * *

Joy

For the next month, Jordan took Allegra out to dinner and lunch, and it was nice getting out again and having someone to talk to. He took the edge off her loneliness and how much she missed Henry. She continued to work on the book, though not quite as much. They went to the movies, and she went to Palm Springs with him for a weekend. They'd been dating for just over a month. It still seemed too fast after Henry, but Jordan made her feel young and alive, and Allegra had decided to accept the theory that you didn't have to be madly in love to have sex, you could enjoy it for what it was. She had never done that before, and liked her old theories better, about only sleeping with a man if she truly loved him, but she was trying to give it a chance.

They bought food on Sunday night when they got back from Palm Springs and ate it in her kitchen. She was feeling more relaxed with him, and getting used to seeing him almost every day. Sometimes he would stop by on his way home from the gym, after Louise had left, and they would race up to her bedroom. And she was starting to believe that he loved her. Maybe it really was possible.

Allegra was clearing away the remains of dinner when she thought Jordan looked odd for a minute, as though he had something to say and wasn't sure when to say it, or how.

"What's up?" she asked him.

"What do you mean?"

"You looked like you were about to say something."

"I . . . well . . . I've been meaning to tell you. I'm starting preproduction on a film soon."

"That's nice. When?"

"I leave in a week, actually," he said, looking uncomfortable.

"To where?" She didn't see his answer coming, or even suspect it.

"London. We're shooting the picture in England."

"The whole picture?" She looked stunned.

"Yeah. The coproducers and investors are British."

"And you'll be gone, what, six months? Plus postproduction."

"Something like that." Jordan looked sheepish, and like a kid again.

"And you didn't tell me? You must have known for the last six months, or three at least. You knew when we started."

"I thought you wouldn't want to get involved if I told you."

"So you just didn't tell me? And now what?"

"I thought you could come over for a couple of weeks sometime this summer," he said.

"A couple of weeks, and you'll be gone six or eight months?" Jordan didn't know how to answer her. She had nailed him. She was too smart. "You supposedly waited nine years for the love of your life, and now you take off, with no warning, and I'm supposed to come over for a couple of weeks? Jordan, I know you. We've been friends for too long. Are you already bored? Did you just want to prove you could get me? Well, you did, and I was starting to believe you. Is this an invitation, or goodbye?"

"Maybe a time out to figure things out and decide if this is really what we want."

"Ahhh, right . . . time-out. Let me tell you something. You don't have to pretend that you've been dreaming of someone for nine years to get them into bed. Even me. You're good at this. Women want to go to bed with you, and they have a great time when they get there. You deliver the goods. You're incredible. You don't have to trick them, and then bullshit them when you run away. I had a terrific time. I probably won't ever do something like this again. Real is better. I think we've done it. And you know it too. Have a great time in England, and good luck with your film." Allegra stood up and waited for him to leave, and Jordan had the grace to be embarrassed. She felt like a fool. She had been one. And she'd fallen for his line, vulnerable because she was lonely and missed Henry so much.

"Allegra, don't be like that. This isn't me. This is heavy stuff, being together all the time. And it's true. I've wanted you since the day I met you."

"You wanted me because Henry had me, and you wanted to be him and have whatever he had. So you had to prove you could get me now. I get it. It's kind of a cheap shot to pull on an old friend. You didn't need to do this, except for your ego. You won. You got me. The sex was fabulous. The bullshit is not so hot. That's not fair. Have a nice trip."

"I'm sorry," he said, and hung his head for a minute. "I'll call you from London," he said hesitantly.

"Don't. I had a lifetime of that before I met Henry. People who make promises they don't keep, who lie, who don't call and don't come back, and don't mean what they say, or don't say anything, and don't care. I thought I was finished with all that, and I was, with Henry. With you, it's just more of the same. Go find someone who believes it, for a month or two. You've never had trouble finding them before." Jordan didn't say a word. Allegra understood him perfectly. There was nothing he could say. She knew the truth, and saw right through him.

He walked out of her kitchen, to the front door, and closed it quietly behind him. What she noticed was that he had forgotten to say goodbye, just like all the others. The good news was that she wasn't in love with him and never had been. She had made a mistake. But she'd get over it. She had to forgive herself, more than him. He was pathetic, and not worth the time, or the tears. She was finished crying over people like him. Henry had healed all those wounds. This had been a stumble, nothing more. Jordan had wasted her time for a month. He hadn't broken her heart. She had known a great love in her life. Jordan was a fraud, as Henry had always suspected. And now she was sure of it.

Chapter 16

The interlude with Jordan only happened once in Allegra's life for a few weeks. It was a reminder of things she already knew. She never heard from him again. She heard that he was back from England nine months later, and judging by the tabloids, the revolving door on his bedroom remained in working order. About two years later, she read that he got married, to a young actress, and divorced a year later. And he'd finally won an Oscar. Allegra had no interest in speaking to him again, and he didn't try either. Simply put, he wasn't real, and never had been.

After the last time Allegra saw Jordan, she went back to work on the book. It took her a year to finish it. She wrote the final words in the book on the second anniversary of Henry's death. It was symbolic. She still missed him terribly, but the book had kept her busy, and him alive in her daily life. She found an agent and a publisher. Pippa read it and loved it, but she didn't edit nonfiction.

The biography of Henry Platt, *Ode to Joy,* came out three years after his death. The movie scores he'd written had become even more famous in that time. He was a legend. And the book had considerable success.

Allegra sent copies of the book to Henry's children, in the hope that they would get to know their father and the kind of man he was through her book. They deserved to know his history, because he was a part of them, and it was their history as well. He was a man to be proud of. She hoped that they read it, although she never heard from them. The poison their mother had filled them with against their father had proved to be fatal to the relationship they had never had with him, and had been an even greater loss for them than for him.

Before the biography came out, Allegra wrote a novel. Her editing skills helped her hone the process. It was a respectable first work of fiction.

In the nine years since his death, she had written the biography and five novels. The last two were firmly on the bestseller list for several weeks, the most recent at number one. She was proud of it, and she thought Henry would have been too. She worked as hard as he had on his music. She had learned that from him, yet another gift he had given her, along with the seven years of their marriage.

She worked night and day on a book until it was finished and did little else. Her books were her life. The characters in them were her family and friends. She had found her path once he was gone. She had been too busy with him to write before that. But at forty-two,

Joy

she was a successful author and led a peaceful life. Her month of madness with Jordan Allen was a unique event she eventually forgave herself for.

She lived in L.A., in the house Henry had left her in Bel Air. Louise still worked for her, although she was threatening to retire. Allegra went to Paris for a week every year in June, on the anniversary of her first trip there with Henry, and stayed at the Ritz. She lived for that trip, and knew the city well now. Her most recent book was set in Paris and included a murder at the Ritz. She had dedicated all of her books to Henry.

Allegra hadn't been seen publicly since her last time, at the Academy Awards with Jordan. Her publisher complained constantly that she didn't do enough press. She hardly did any, except for the rare telephone interview, or a Q&A by email. She remained a mystery to most of her readers, which she preferred. She thought the books should stand on their own, without her exposing herself to the media. Her life was comfortable the way it was. She had no desire to discuss her life, her childhood, or her marriages.

She had just started a new book, a month after finishing the last one. She had worked late the night before, the way Henry used to, and she had just gotten started with a mug of coffee sitting next to her when Louise came to tell her that there was a man named Galen Fairchild on the phone. Allegra didn't recognize the name. Louise knew Allegra hated interruptions when she was writing, but it was still early in the book. She had just started it a few days before. Louise knew not to disturb her when she was trying to finish one.

"I don't know him," Allegra said vaguely, without looking up from her computer. "Find out what he wants and take a message. Tell him

I'm writing." She usually checked her messages at the end of a day's work, or Louise put them on her meal trays. She found Galen Fairchild's when she ate a sandwich for lunch. It said he was from *The New York Times*. Allegra groaned when she read it. Occasionally, she wished she had an assistant, but most of the time she didn't need one.

Allegra debated about returning the call after lunch. He probably wanted an interview, which she wouldn't give him. But reporters were persistent, and he'd call again. It was easier to get it over with and scare him off now. She took particular pleasure in doing that, and confirming her reputation as a recluse. Jordan had cured her of wanting to try "dating" again. She'd probably just get herself in trouble, or fall for someone like him. No one would measure up to Henry. She'd been lucky once, but didn't want to try her luck again. She'd had a great love, and now she had a career, which was going well. It was enough for her.

She picked up the phone and called the number Louise had written down. It was an L.A. number. A man answered, and she asked for Galen Fairchild by name. He came on the line immediately. He had a deep pleasant voice and sounded cheerful and friendly.

Allegra said who she was, and he thanked her for returning the call. "I work for *The New York Times*," he explained. "I cover books and authors in the L.A. area. I read your biography of your husband recently and loved it. And I just read your latest novel, and I love that too. I've admired your husband's work for years. And I have a particular fondness for Paris. I studied there for a year, so you hooked me with the location and the Ritz. And now here I am. I'm told you

JOY

don't do interviews," he said, sounding amused. "But I thought I'd give it a shot and see if you'd talk to me. It's for the Sunday magazine. Full profile. Good for book sales," he said, hoping to be convincing, while she hesitated.

"It's true, I don't do interviews, and I just started a new book. Maybe in six or eight months, we could talk sometime," she said vaguely, hoping to fob him off, and he laughed.

"Oh, cruel woman," he said, "what do I tell my editor?"

"That I'm a cranky pain in the ass, and I wouldn't talk to you. You can lie and tell them you couldn't reach me." He laughed again.

"Wait, let me write that down . . . cranky pain in the ass . . . Why don't you like interviews, by the way?"

"Because I have nothing to say. I don't think interviews are relevant. I could be psychotic and it doesn't matter, if the book is any good. And my private life is my business, not the public's."

"All true. You don't sound psychotic."

"I'm not. Just cranky, and private. My late husband was too."

"I know. He really was a remarkable person," Fairchild said admiringly. "You portrayed that beautifully. I fell in love with him, reading your book." They had sent him a review copy.

"Me too. He was a very special person." Her voice softened when she said it, and filled with emotion.

"Would you have coffee with me? Entirely off the record, not an interview. Maybe we could figure out something you'd want to talk about. Paris maybe. I just think your readers deserve to know more about you. I got the feeling that the woman who wrote about Henry Platt was special too. You understood all the nuances of his artistic persona. That's a real talent, and being able to write about it and convey it to the reader is another one. You write well, and you're a brilliant observer of the human species."

"Not always," she said, thinking of Jordan Allen. "I've been fascinated by people since I was a kid. I used to think I was invisible, that I could see them and they couldn't see me." Fairchild knew it was the sign of an unhappy childhood, but he didn't say that to her. He'd had a drunken father as a child, and had been severely beaten by him, as had his mother. He survived it, she didn't. She had died of a fractured skull when he was ten, and his father had gone to prison. Galen Fairchild had been placed in an orphanage, and had been lucky when a loving couple in Boston had adopted him six months after his mother died, and changed his life. He would never have survived without them. They had taken him to Paris and he had fallen in love with it. They had been like fairy godparents in his life, and had opened the world up to him.

"I was invisible for a while too," Galen Fairchild shared with Allegra. "It was hard to pull off though. I have red hair." She laughed when he said it.

"So do I," she said, smiling.

"I know, from the photos on the back of your books. So, should we be invisible and have coffee? Would you trust me for one cup, if you can get away from the book you're writing?" She hesitated. She really didn't want to meet him, but he sounded like a decent guy. Few reporters were, in her opinion.

"I hate being interrupted," she growled at him.

"You don't have to do the interview," he said. "The cup of coffee doesn't obligate you. And you can do the interview a year from now, or whenever your next book comes out, if you want to. Your publisher will like that." It was true, and he was persistent, gently but doggedly so.

"You're very persuasive for an invisible guy with red hair," she said, and he laughed.

"Who knows, maybe we'll wind up friends. Stranger things have happened. I usually like my subjects. I can't write about them if I don't."

"I have to like the characters in my books," she shared with him.

"You're lucky. I want to write a book one day. I have no time now with my job."

"Eleven o'clock tomorrow morning." Allegra gave him the name of a deli she went to occasionally, where no one paid attention to her.

"I'll be there." He jotted it down. "And thank you. We can make it quick."

"I want to be at my desk by noon," she said firmly.

"I'll get up and leave mid-sentence at eleven forty-five." He knew she lived in Bel Air. "See you tomorrow, and thank you." Galen Fairchild had a gentle voice, and there was something about him she liked. She wasn't sure why, since he was a journalist, and she had a deep suspicion of them.

Allegra was about to put on a gray sweatshirt and jeans the next morning after she showered, and she stared at her red hair in the mirror. It looked a mess, and she brushed it. It hung straight down her back, and she put on black jeans and a white sweater, just to make some small effort. She didn't want to be one of those authors who tried to look their worst to prove that they were intellectuals.

She put gold earrings on as she rushed out the door and got in her car.

She got to the deli five minutes early and waited in her car until she saw him. She didn't want to sit in the restaurant alone. She was still shy, and even more so once Henry was gone, and no longer there to protect her. She had felt so safe with him for those magical seven years. Now she was alone again and had to protect herself.

Allegra was surprised by Galen Fairchild's size. He was very tall, with broad shoulders. He looked like a big teddy bear. She noticed the red hair immediately. He was wearing a blue shirt, a blazer, jeans, and loafers. He looked like he came from the East Coast, and had the right look for a reporter from *The New York Times*. Respectable. Traditional. Old-school.

She walked into the deli a minute after he did, and he smiled down at her. She felt tiny next to him, although she wasn't. She guessed him to be about six four.

"You were watching me," he said with a smile, amused.

"How do you know that?" she asked him, and he pointed to her hair.

"I saw you in your car. You're not as invisible as you think. Neither am I. I was six four by the time I was fifteen. That's hard to hide, with the hair."

They got their coffee and sat down, and she asked him where he was from.

"Boston." They talked about Paris and the East Coast, and she told him about the cottage in Newport. He had been there once. He said he loved Los Angeles and had lived there for five years. He told her

Joy

he was divorced and had no kids. He had gone to Yale, and was an English literature major, as she had been. He told her he was adopted, and she sensed that there was a story there. They both had their histories. He said that he and his ex-wife were good friends. She had remarried and had four kids, and he was godfather to one of them.

"I didn't want kids, so we split, and she found the right guy after me."

"I didn't want them either. I didn't want to give someone a miserable childhood if I made mistakes," she confessed.

"Yeah, me too, something like that. The sins of the father, and all that." She knew exactly what he meant. She had worried that she would be a mother like her own. What if it was in their DNA? Galen Fairchild was two years older than she was, though they looked about the same age. She vaguely remembered that he was forty-three. She had looked him up on Google. He stood up then while they were talking and looked at his watch. "Time's up." She was startled and then she remembered their deal, and smiled as she stood up too. "You have to go back to your desk or you won't talk to me again." She probably wouldn't anyway, and decided to be honest with him as they left the deli.

"I'm not going to do the interview, you know."

"I figured." He didn't look surprised. "I just wanted to meet you. Your books are so interesting. I love them, I'm reading your second novel now." She laughed.

"I was curious too," Allegra admitted. She liked him. He seemed normal and real, and it sounded like he might have had a rough road too to get where he was. Not wanting kids was a clue. She suspected they had more in common than red hair. But he wasn't angry or bitter. And he loved Paris, so he couldn't be all bad. She hadn't taken a risk on anyone in nine years, since Henry died, and wondered if it was time. She hadn't even considered it since Jordan and hadn't missed it. The books had filled her time. But some of what Jordan had said was true. She needed a life. And the books weren't enough. She needed real people in her life too. The books were her escape into a fantasy life, and had been since her childhood. She read them then. Now she wrote them.

Galen Fairchild walked Allegra to her car. She felt dwarfed beside him. "Can I call you again?" he asked her.

"I told you I won't do the interview," she reminded him.

"I know. I heard you. I meant for lunch or dinner sometime. Just me, no interview. Invisible dining," he said, and she laughed. "Or maybe I could meet you in Paris for lunch. All my favorite restaurants are there. Although I know a nice little French place on Melrose that's pretty authentic. Cassoulet, hachis parmentier, confit de canard, boudin noir. French bistro food. The real deal." He seemed like the real deal too, not just because of the food he liked. She could sense that he was an honorable man and a straightforward person.

"That would be nice," Allegra said. She'd been running for a long time, and wondered if it was time to stop. It was tiring, running from the world alone, and not a lot of fun. Galen seemed like he might be interesting. She didn't know what had made her agree to meet him, but something had. Destiny maybe, or blind luck, like when she'd gone to interview with Henry for a job, and a whole new world opened up to her after that.

Joy

"Call you in eight months when you finish the book?" he said, with a hopeful tone of voice and a twinkle in his eye.

"Maybe in three or four weeks, after I get the outline worked out," she said, and he nodded, pleased. He had the strong feeling that they had met for a reason, and so did she.

"That'll work. I'm free in eight months too, if you lose track of time. I know how writers are," he said, and she laughed out loud. "I'm going to tell them you wouldn't take my call, by the way. They'll leave you alone and won't assign anyone else to you, for a while anyway."

"Thank you." Allegra felt an unseen thread that connected them as she looked at Galen. It was a powerful bond of some kind. He felt it too. Maybe similarities in their histories, or something comparable.

"Thank you for coming to meet me," he said, as she got into her car and looked up at him.

"See you soon," Allegra said, and knew she would. Galen stepped back and she waved as she drove away. She could see him in the rearview mirror as he got in his own car, a battered Jeep. He was smiling, and as she drove back to Bel Air, she realized the most precious legacy Henry had left her. She had put it away for a long time and tried to forget it. But it had bubbled back up to the surface and she could feel it rising up inside her. It was joy. And when you added love to it, magic happened. That was what Henry had left her to keep with her forever. She remembered it now. Joy. No one could take it away from her. It was deep within her, and no one could deprive her of it. She had sensed joy in Galen too, and kindness, and courage. It took courage to hang on to joy, and determination not to lose it. The bad people and the bad times made one grow stronger and appreciate joy even more when one found it again, still intact, its light shining even brighter than before. She was looking forward to seeing Galen again. And whatever happened, she had joy in her soul. She had found it again, deep within her, brighter and stronger than ever.

About the Author

DANIELLE STEEL has been hailed as one of the world's bestselling authors, with a billion copies of her novels sold. Her many international bestsellers include *Resurrection, Only the Brave, Never Too Late, Upside Down, The Ball at Versailles, Second Act, Happiness, Palazzo,* and other highly acclaimed novels. She is also the author of *His Bright Light,* the story of her son Nick Traina's life and death; *A Gift of Hope,* a memoir of her work with the homeless; *Expect a Miracle,* a book of her favorite quotations for inspiration and comfort; *Pure Joy,* about the dogs she and her family have loved; and the children's books *Pretty Minnie in Paris* and *Pretty Minnie in Hollywood.*

daniellesteel.com
Facebook.com/DanielleSteelOfficial
X: @daniellesteel
Instagram: @officialdaniellesteel

About the Type

This book was set in Charter, a typeface designed in 1987 by Matthew Carter (b. 1937) for Bitstream, Inc., a digital typefoundry that he cofounded in 1981. One of the most influential typographers of our time, Carter designed this versatile font to feature a compact width, squared serifs, and open letterforms. These features give the typeface a fresh, highly legible, and unencumbered appearance.